# MOURNING SICKNESS

## A BENTON FALLS MYSTERY
### BOOK TWO

## BRIAN DELANEY

Mourning Sickness
A Benton Falls Mystery- Book Two



ISBNs:
979-8-9852578-4-7 (print)
979-8-9852578-5-4 (eBook)

# DEDICATION

I dedicate this novel to my dear friend and beta reader, the late Jim Puckey.

*A tree gives shade from the hot sun to whomever lies beneath. But if you think about it, the tree does so at the cost of taking the heat onto itself. The tree is selfless and charitable. It is unyielding in its commitment to shield, steadfast in its responsibility to aid those beneath its branches.*

-Japanese proverb

Jim, you were one hell of a tree. Like the mighty oak, you protected, offered comfort, showed strength, and proved your unselfishness to all who knew you.

Thank you for your shade, Jim.

Two months after Harley Benton, last in the bloodline from the founder of Benton Falls, had a stroke, a woman walked through the sliding doors of the Benton Falls Assisted Living and Memory Care Center (FALM) and shook the raindrops from her umbrella before depositing it in the nearby stand. Taking off her raincoat and placing it over her arm, she stepped up to the desk, pushing an errant strand of hair from her vision before greeting Dottie Selzak, the new receptionist.

"Good afternoon," the woman said as she signed in to visit Berta Hendricks, housed in the wing known as the Passing Lane. Nicknamed by the staff, this section of the FALM was designed to keep the incapable, comatose, terminally ill, and end-of-life residents away from the more robust elderly population to make certain death didn't come as a complete surprise to anyone in the building. Those patients who entered this wing rarely left on anything other than a stretcher.

On the arm opposite to holding her raincoat, the woman carried a large bag with looped handles and opened it for Dottie to inspect. Flowers overflowed the space above the bag with a sweet scent.

The visitor, dressed in nurse scrubs, was in her late fifties. Her brown hair was mottled with the emergence of grey streaks framing the crow's feet around her eyes, crinkling otherwise smooth skin. The weight she'd put on disguised the fact she once owned an hourglass figure. All aging signs masked indications that this had once been a stunning young woman.

Dottie nodded and gave her a visitor sticker. The woman put down the bag and placed the yellow sticker against her scrubs pocket away from her raincoat to prevent moisture from affecting its adhesiveness.

Showing her authority, Dottie called after the woman, "Calling hours end at seven pm sharp!" The visitor felt the receptionist's eyes on her back as she entered the Passing Lane, knowing that Dottie would check the register for her name. She wasn't wrong. *Arabella Fischer.*

Walking down the hallway, Ms. Fischer stopped at room one-sixty-five and stepped in. The most recent occupant for the time being was Mrs. Hendricks, her residency in the Passing Lane soon coming to an end.

No matter, thought the visitor. *I won't be long.* The room smelled of disinfectant and the decay of the elderly. Two fragrances Arabella was familiar with as a nurse, yet still made her cringe.

Mrs. Hendricks lay unconscious and couldn't carry on a conversation, so Arabella would need not linger, having other business to attend to. The flowers were a nice touch, though.

Taking the bouquet from the bag, she placed the vase on the nightstand, waiting patiently for five minutes before slipping out of the room, glad to be away from the stench. Being familiar with something and tolerating it were two different things. She would never get used to the smell of oncoming death.

The visitor walked to the next door, room one sixty-seven, opened it slowly, and slipped in, making sure the door closed quietly behind her.

"Hello, old man," she whispered, rousing the patient in the bed from an early evening nap. His right eye opened, while the left drooped. His right hand lifted as if to offer a wave or to signal stop; she ignored both messages. The left hand lay immobile on the bed as if waiting to be summoned.

"Up for a visitor?" she asked cheerfully, walking to the side of the bed, and depositing the bag on a chair near the window. Harley Benton was now fully awake and staring at the woman, trying to speak but the words were replaced by garbled and unintelligible sounds.

Arabella sat on the bed and grabbed his good hand, its coldness contrasted with her warmth. "Are you going to lie in this godforsaken place forever?" she asked, expecting no response. "I thought it was a good time to come visit and see what plans you had for the future."

The old man lay still, glaring warily at the woman with his one good eye the way a hiker might size up a wildlife threat.

"I know, I know. I should have come sooner," she offered. "But I'm here now, so doesn't that count for something?" When Benton continued his stare, she commented, "OK, I'll fess up. It shouldn't surprise you what I'm capable of when the flow of money ceases, should it? I got rather anxious when the checks stopped coming. I chalked up the first missed one to you being forgetful. But the second missed check? I knew there was a problem. So, I did some snooping and discovered your butler and the Ahearne fella have taken over your business. They must have canceled my checks. This can't sit well with you, can it?"

Still silent, Benton gave her the impression he was scowling on the inside.

"Didn't think so," she said. "It doesn't sit well with me either. Especially when the future for our family looks so bright." When the old man raised his right eyebrow she added, "After you're gone, I mean, sweetie. *After* you're gone. We all know who's still in charge. But the balance of power is shifting. Consider this a new partnership. I help you, and you help me." Rising, she pulled a small black case from the flower bag and placed it on the bed.

"So, I have a solution for all of us," she said, waving the case. "And it starts with a new drug that fights inflammation in autoimmune patients." When Benton tilted his head, Arabella continued.

"You know, like arthritis. Well, this drug shows promise in testing with stroke patients. The research suggests it helps to ease the inflammation of the brain." She lifted upturned hands toward him, questioning, "Has your doctor even mentioned this drug? It's called Flomatient. Terrible name. Sounds like a urinary tract medication."

Benton gave a small shake of his head.

"There are trials out there but the American Academy of Neurology is saying there is insufficient evidence for use on stroke patients and warns of side effects."

Benton shrugged his right shoulder. "Does this mean you'd like to try it?" she asked, rewarded by a nod from the old man.

Tilting her head to one side, "And the side effects?"

Benton dropped his head and again raised the right eyebrow. Arabella took that to mean the side effects for an 80-year-old man wouldn't matter as long as it improved his condition for the short term. *What did the old codger have left to lose?*

Benton coughed, forcing Arabella to grab a tissue from the box on the nightstand and put it against the old man's mouth causing a slight string of phlegm to arc as she took it away.

"I see your lung function is improving," she said, surveying the small amount of sputum. "At least your doctor got one thing right." This comment was in response to the medication he was on limiting the amount of mucous he *used* to spit up. She'd been around a myriad of patients with unpleasant bodily fluids but just the thought of that nasty business made her cringe. Throwing away the tissue, she gathered this was one medication Benton had no problem ingesting.

"Ok, then," she said, opening the case and pulling out a vial and syringe. "It took me this long to get my hands on enough of this drug to be effective. Of course, this treatment goes along with your physical therapy. Won't help you walk but should give you some of your speech back and possibly limited mobility. And we're going to need you to communicate effectively for the next part of the plan. Getting you out of here… and ousting the vermin at Benton Manor."

Filling the syringe, she put an arm behind Benton's back and pushed him forward. "Sorry for the prick, but let's see if we can't get you into fighting shape. You're going to need it for what's coming," she apologized, before injecting the needle between two vertebrae and plunging.

Withdrawing the needle, she gently laid the man back against his pillow. Once he was comfortable, Arabella sat on the edge of the bed. "You helped me all these years, it's time I returned the favor, so here's the plan." She leaned in and began to whisper. The old man's eye grew larger, a half-smile forming on his face accomplished by extreme will. It was much too early for the drug to take effect.

Knowing he approved of her plan, she gazed down at him and shook her head. "Boy, aging kicked your ass, didn't it? I can't stop the progress, just improve it a bit." While she put her medical supplies away, she continued speaking. "And getting your estate returned will make things more comfortable. Sleeping in your own bed sounds nice, doesn't it?"

She didn't wait for him to respond, but she did change her tone. "But it's going to cost you, old man. Getting a monthly check all these years has been nice, but what I'm proposing doesn't come without risks. I'll need to be fairly compensated for those risks. Don't you agree?"

Benton nodded once more, albeit slowly.

"Not quite good enough, I think." She took a pen and a small pad out of the flower bag and handed both to the old man.

"Let's also get back at those fools who thought they could take something belonging to the great Harley Benton."

Benton used his right hand to write out one word. Arabella spun the pad around. The word was chicken scratched but still readable: *Yes.*

"Good, now that we understand each other, I think it's time for me to leave. I'll be back soon for more doses and check on your progress, but this is our little secret. You must be patient and *quiet* until the time is right, understand?"

Harley Benton nodded once more and pointed to the pad she held.

"Excellent," she said, changing her tone back to cheerful. Picking up her bag, she leaned over to kiss the old man on the forehead, noticing his eye never left her face.

"We really should spring you from this place soon. It smells," she said, wrinkling her nose. "But all in good time, Harley. All in good time."

She walked around the bed and headed for the door. Grabbing the door handle, she turned towards him. "Oh, by the way, you're going to get a visitor soon. I'm sure you two will become fast friends. But remember, mum's the word until we're ready," she announced, a single finger pressed against her lips.

Opening the door with her bag hand, she exclaimed, "Toodles!" while waving her fingers at him as if playing keys on a piano. She then slipped out into the hallway.

Glad to be leaving the Passing Lane, Arabella sported a grin filled with the knowledge she'd left Harley Benton's head filled with thoughts of going home to Benton Manor…and revenge.

# Chapter One

(Four months later)

"Veronica, you're going to put me in an early grave with this kind of talk." Winnie Ahearne rocked slowly on the front porch of her old, and now, Veronica's new home.

For the time being.

Veronica Bucholz ignored the comment as she rocked in her own chair, noticing how the early evening sun had dipped behind the tree-lined street, the start of the evening ritual of casting shadows that danced across the front yard. The forecast was for rain later and clouds were building in the distance, so she needed to get Winnie home soon.

"Jesus, Mary, and Joseph, and all the bald-headed angels, I swear I'm gonna need a belt of the 'ol Irish to calm my nerves," Winnie said.

Despite the difficult conversation, Veronica smiled at the old woman's phrase. "Where on earth did you get that saying?"

"I picked it up from my grandfather, long since dead. I'm not sure if it's taking the lord's name in vain, so just to stay on the safe side…." She made the sign of the cross and looked heavenward as if for absolution.

"But why bald-headed? Babies have hair when born, why not angels? Or are angels just old and have lost their hair?" Veronica teased, but Winnie wasn't in the mood.

The old lady groused, "It's to keep the halo straight on their angelic heads. Hair gets in the way of a perfect halo."

"If I were an angel, I'd be fashionable. I'd tilt my halo to the side. Like an English woman's fascinator." Veronica giggled at the thought.

"If you were an angel, you most certainly would not!" Winnie barked. "And you'd know that if you spent more time in church." With her reprimand, the old woman had turned the mood sour. The two sat in silence before Winnie broke it. "Speaking of babies, What about when yours comes? Who will be in California to help you? Have you thought this through?"

"Winnie," Veronica responded. "I have thought about a lot of things. It's not that I don't appreciate all the support, I do. But I don't think I can stay here. I see Leif everywhere I go and the pain becomes too much for me to handle. I'm drowning here."

Veronica watched as Winnie cringed at the thought of her dead grandson, Veronica's boyfriend, and the father to her unborn child.

Winnie's tone softened. "Vee, isn't remembering him a good thing? I don't ever want to forget him."

Veronica stopped rocking and looked squarely at Winnie. "Sometimes it is a good thing. I remember how he made me laugh. Held me in his arms. How he loved me."

"Well, there you go. Blessed are the couples, for they shall stay with their family."

Winnie had a habit of messing up the Beatitudes or just making up new ones. Veronica smiled softly, but a sadness lurked behind it. When she moved away from Benton Falls, she would surely miss the town and everyone here. Especially Winnie and her odd expressions.

Reaching her hand out and placing it on Winnie's arm, Veronica explained further, "Please try and understand. Those 'good things' come with a cost. Everywhere I go, I'm reminded of Leif and what a good life lay ahead for us. But he's gone and the good life we shared is as well. I used to be happy, confident, *optimistic.* And try as I might, the only thing I feel is sadness. All the time. And that is not healthy for me or…" she patted her pregnant belly. "*That's* why I need to leave. I need a fresh start. I need peace. We both do."

Winnie sighed. "Well, can you get me a sip of the Irish to calm my nerves before taking me back to the FALM? I don't want the residents to see me tipple. And we can discuss this topic further at dinner tomorrow night."

"Sure," said Veronica as she slowly struggled to pull herself out of the rocker before heading to the kitchen. Discussing this topic further was the last thing she wanted but she hated seeing Winnie in distress. Hadn't the old woman seen enough loss in her lifetime? First, her son and daughter-in-law were lost in a car accident many years ago. Leif died earlier this year. Even though still amongst the living, Axel and Jules were traipsing all over the country hyping Leif's books. And now she wanted to leave, taking Winnie's only great-grandchild with her.

Veronica poured a shot into a tumbler, then added another for good measure. Winnie deserved a treat. She'd been working so hard as General Manager of the FALM and this news just caused more grief. Plus, it might help her sleep.

"Don't falter now," she whispered. Family or not, she had to leave. She didn't want to erase the memory of her dead boyfriend, but merely direct her focus on moving forward. If not for herself, then for the child growing inside her.

Walking back onto the porch, she handed the tumbler to the old woman. Winnie sniffed it before taking a sip. Smacking her lips, she asked, "Have you decided on a timeline yet?"

"I'm just beginning to research, so no. I'm focused on two goals. My first task is to get a job. I have a few places that interest me. My second task is finding a place to live."

Winnie finished her drink and laid the glass on the table next to the rocker. "I believe it's about time you took me back to the FALM. I have a lot of work to do tomorrow." Sighing, the old woman said in resignation, "Looks like you have a plan."

"I do, Winnie. I really do." Both women took their time lifting themselves from the rockers before walking down the porch stairs to the driveway. Shooting concerned glances at each other when they heard the sound of thunder in the distance, they shuffled quickly toward the car.

As they drove towards the FALM, neither woman knew it at the time, but when it came to Veronica's two goals, she would accomplish neither.

The next day's weather was raw and gray. More cold rain threatened yet scared no one in Benton Falls. This was typical autumn weather. The leaves turned. Then the rain came, knocking them off their branches, floating to the ground to rot. The circle of life.

It was now late in the afternoon as Winnie hung up the phone and sat at her desk rubbing her knuckles, the pain from her arthritis adding to her already uncomfortable position. She listened to the rain pelt her office window as she recalled the part of her dead grandson's eulogy, delivered by her very much alive one, Axel. *Do you know what happens to a Leif in a tree? They always fall.* Leif had fallen and no one caught him.

"Jesus, Mary, and Joseph, and all the bald-headed angels," she said to an empty office, sighing. "I'm way too old for this crap."

She heard the scream of an ambulance siren approaching and hoped it wasn't coming for *another* one of her residents. Mr. James Granger, housed in the Passing Lane, had expired during the night. She didn't need another death today and was relieved when the siren faded into the distance. As general manager of the Benton Falls Assisted Living and Memory Care Center or FALM for short, Winnie was responsible for overseeing the health and well-being of the residents and staff. A promise she made to grandson Axel after he was named executor of the estate of an incapacitated Harley Benton, now a resident under Winnie's care.

By most standards, Winnie *was* old. At an age when most people slowed down ten years prior, at seventy-eight, she felt she was still sharp of mind and spry of body. To her, age was just a number and she didn't view hers as old. However, some expressed concern because of her lapses in memory, names forgotten, and a habit of confusing common sayings.

Normally she would comment, "Let others worry. If they haven't the sense to mind their own business, they deserve the stress." But lately, especially after Leif's passing, it was she who worried. Her concern began with her grandson, Axel, and his girlfriend, Jules, on the road performing seminars and selling Leif's book on self-help. She fretted about her chief of security, Hector Gonzalez. He was young and capable, but she watched over him in a motherly fashion. The bothersome niggling that followed her around wondering which residents would be next to enter the Passing Lane. She was concerned about the soul of her late grandson Leif. He had strayed from the Christian faith yet had selflessly chosen to save her life from a confused and demented soul but lost his own in the process. Would this final noble act make up for his past sins? She hoped so but couldn't be sure.

She heard a distant rumble of thunder. It was as if God was answering her in the negative, adding to her concerns.

With worry came fatigue. Having worked in her own restaurant for years, one would have thought she would take it easy. Glide through retirement. But no. She had a promise to keep and although she did enjoy most of the work the FALM provided, she could do without days like today.

It began with the news of Mr. Granger's passing. Death was nothing new to Winnie. And this year had been no exception. At her age, most of her friends were all well into the hereafter.

The old man's death coupled with the inclement weather seemed to darken everyone's mood, causing increased resident squabbles and hurt feelings to soothe. Finally, Winnie's over-protective nature kicked in when it concerned the remaining living family members.

"Where is she?" Winnie asked out loud while staring at the phone as if it would ring any second. She picked up the receiver and dialed again. And again, like the previous attempts all day, the call went to voicemail. Winnie hung up.

She picked up the receiver again and called her security chief, Hector Gonzalez.

"Hector?' she began, "I'm a little concerned."

"Yes, Miss Winnie, how can I help you?"

Winnie thought before speaking. She decided it was too early to concern Hector about her fear, so she shifted gears. "Have you made the arrangements for Mr. Granger yet?" she asked.

"Yes, Ma'am. I called Cullen's this morning. All taken care of. So no need for concern."

One of her first duties as general manager was to cut costs. Even though Cullen's Funeral Home had been the family's choice for years, she had a sit down with Pat Cullen. He was a hard bargainer, but when confronted with Winnie's choice between her way or the highway, he relented.

"And how was it out on the floor today?" She already knew the answer. Dottie had filled her in. Death days were always a bit dicey at the FALM as the healthy residents were forced to contemplate their own mortality. Watching one of their own leave the building for the last time on a sheet-covered stretcher put everyone on edge.

"This morning was tough on the residents," Hector answered. "But this afternoon has been quiet except for the Visiting Angels today."

"Well, that's a good thing." The residents always looked forward to visits from the church group of which Axel had been a part. "Let's hope it stays quiet through seven p.m.," said Winnie. The clock across from her desk read four o'clock.

Three more hours until what she referred to as the 'bewitching hour,' when visiting came to an end and the residents began their nightly ritual of slowing down and heading to their rooms.

"Miss Winnie?" Hector asked. "Is everything all right? You sound tired."

"Hector, always looking out for this old woman," she answered. "No, everything is fine." She felt bad about lying to Hector but felt it was too early to pass on the worry. Just yet. "I've got a little paperwork to finish up before I head to my room. Thanks for asking. Good night."

This would be one night when Winnie was glad she lived on the premises. Axel wouldn't let her drive anymore and it *was* a short commute to and from her office. Another thunder rumble made its presence known. This time closer. An oncoming storm provided a second reason to be glad she lived at the FALM.

Winnie didn't actually believe she was too old for the job as FALM Manager. She maintained a healthy worry for the residents and staff, an unhealthy one to make sure what had transpired, the *hastenings*, would never happen again, and a concern for her living grandson Axel and his girlfriend Jules. She wished they'd come off the road and return to Benton Falls, not knowing exactly where they were on the West Coast. San Diego? Portland? Seattle?

There was enough to worry about at the FALM. It came with the job description. One final element had her worried to the point of fear and caused her weariness. She could handle those other worries, but this one truly terrified her. She picked up the receiver and tried once again to reach her… her what? her granddaughter? Her friend? She wasn't sure what to call Leif's pregnant girlfriend. They were going to get engaged the night Leif was killed. Even though the girl wasn't connected by marriage, she was connected by something stronger. A great-grandchild. Winnie had tried all day to reach out to her to no avail. All she got was her voicemail. Just like this one.

Slowly, Winnie placed the phone back in its cradle. Then laid her head on the desk as the weariness overtook her. She tried to rationalize it by suggesting options. The girl was working late at the hospital and as a nurse, meant long hours. Perhaps her phone died? Or maybe she was at a place where she couldn't use it?

Despite these possible scenarios, the worry and fear persisted. Winnie lifted her head and looked once more at the phone. As if to add to her concerns, a flash of light was followed by a loud thunderclap, as rain once again began to pelt her office window.

"Dammit, Veronica, where the hell are you?" she asked before again placing her weary head on the desk. *Way too old…*

At six forty-five, fifteen minutes until Winnie's 'bewitching hour,' a young man entered the FALM and went straight to the front desk to sign in. He ran a hand through his wet hair, a victim of the latest rainstorm. He unsuccessfully attempted to dry his hands on his wet trousers and looking up, smiled sheepishly at the receptionist.

"Sir," began Dottie, looking at the big clock on the wall opposite her station, "You do know visiting hours are over in fifteen minutes?" Dottie hated it when late visitors came in. Some scofflaws would stay past the curfew, causing her to play the bad cop and kick them out. *Why doesn't everyone play by the rules?*

"I understand," replied the young man, shaking his hands of the excess moisture. The drops made tiny circles on the floor by his feet. "I promise I won't be long. Just want to say hello to a family friend."

Pushing a box of tissues toward the young man Dottie said, "OK, just sign here and who you're visiting."

The young man wiped his hands with a tissue before placing it on the desk. Dottie picked it up with pinched fingers and dropped it into a basket at her feet, wearing a disgusted look suggesting the young man had just used it to blow a runny nose.

After he signed the register, he spun it around for the nurse to see. Her eyes looked over her glasses at the young man as she bit the inside of her lip. "He's in room one sixty-seven in the Pass…." Catching herself, she began again. "He's in room one sixty-seven. That way." She pointed the young man in the right direction, reminding him of the time by tapping a finger on her left wrist. "Fifteen minutes. Don't make me come after you."

Once he was out of sight, she picked up the phone.

"Hector, this is Dottie. You are not going to believe what just happened. Can you come to the front desk?"

"Sure," Hectored answered. "Be right there."

Dottie was looking at the signature on the register, *Will Ames,* as Hector came up to the desk. "Dottie, what's up?"

"This young man just came in for a visit… Couldn't have been more than twenty-eight or nine. Why would he be visiting *that resident,* for god's sake?"

"It's ten minutes to seven," Hector said, interrupting the receptionist. Everyone at the FALM knew she loved to gossip. He was uninterested in hearing any.

"I explained this but he said he'd only be a few moments."

Hector pursed his lips. "So, what's the problem?" he said, the tone of exasperation evident.

"It's not his lateness. It's who he came to see that surprised me. *Room one sixty-seven.*" Dottie spun the sign-in sheet around so Hector could see the signature of the visitor and the name of the visited. His eyes grew wide. *Now* he was interested.

"He hasn't had a visitor since he got here," he said, scratching his temple.

"At least not since I've been here," replied Dottie. "It's exactly why I called you."

"Why would a visitor, a young man at that, come to see the old man?"

Dottie pointed towards the hallway as the young man appeared. "Why don't you ask him yourself?"

"I told you I wouldn't be long. Ask me what?" the young man said as he approached the front desk.

Hector took a deep breath. "We were just wondering why?"

"Why?" said the young man. "Why what?"

Hector looked over at Dottie. She nodded toward the head of FALM security as if to say, *Go ahead. It's your job. So, ask.*

Hector turned back towards the young man and did his job.

"We just wanted to know why you came tonight to visit the man in room one sixty-seven?"

The room's occupant was Mr. Harley Benton.

"Did you have any trouble?" asked the person behind the window on the second floor of the building. His voice was deep and gravelly, like an old man. The window was oversized and covered with film, making it opaque, appearing out of place in an office so tiny. On the side of the office was a small hallway attached to the exterior wall.

On the ground floor, two men stood on either side of a chair. Seated in between them was a woman in a long raincoat with a sleeping mask covering her eyes. She mumbled but was unintelligible because the men who had abducted her placed duct tape over her mouth.

"Not really boss. Grabbed her at her house early this morning before anyone in the neighborhood woke up," said the man on the right.

"Like you told us, there was a lot of tree cover along the driveway. Plus, it was raining. Nobody could have seen us, no way," replied the man on the left before adding, "She threatened us the police would come looking for her if she didn't show up for work so as a precaution, I used her phone to text her supervisor that she was calling in sick. Smart, eh?"

"Her supervisor?" asked the old man. "Winnie Ahearne doesn't have a supervisor. She *is* the supervisor. Please tell me you have the phone?" Grizz, the larger of the two, patted himself down looking for the cell phone he didn't possess. "Must've dropped it," he said weakly. When Grizz looked at his feet, a loud sigh was audible.

"Pinky, please take off her mask," ordered the man from above. "Leave the tape."

Pinky was the small man on the right. A lifelong criminal, he, and his partner Grizz, so named for his blond hair and large size and, clearly the muscle for the two, had been offered a job to kidnap a woman. And damn lucky to get this gig after the shit show in New York. They worked for dangerous men and

Pinky felt their screwup back east was the end of the line for them both until this job fell into their laps.

They were unaware of whom they now worked for; the man above shielded by the film-tinted window. They only heard his voice from speakers situated around the almost empty building. In their line of work, it was not uncommon to work for an unidentified person. And safer too, as long as they were referred by someone they could trust. Like one of their 'friends.'

Gratitude they were given a second chance and an advance on their fee guaranteed no questions were asked. But neither did it stop their silent suppositions.

"Yes sir." Pinky obliged by removing the mask. "See, we got her!"

The young woman looked up and squinted at the voice behind the window, her eyes adjusting to the light.

Grizz jumped in. "Do we get paid now or is there somethin' else we can do for you?"

There was another sigh from above. The voice spoke quietly but with a hint of malice.

"Gentleman, who were you supposed to abduct?"

Pinky reached into his pocket and pulled out a piece of paper. He read, "Winnie Ahearne, 430 Willow Road, Benton Falls."

"That is the correct address. However, if you take the tape off the young lady, you'll find out she is not the right target." The voice coughed before finishing. "Go ahead, Pinky. Take the tape off."

Pinky did as he was told, but not gently.

"Dammit, that hurt!" yelled Veronica Bucholtz. "Who the hell are you guys and what do you want?"

The voice answered from above, "I apologize for the inconvenience, young lady. There has been a mistake. It seems as though my friends here brought me the wrong woman." Then addressing Pinky and Grizz, he added, "Gentlemen, this is a *young* woman. Winnie Ahearne is an *old* woman. Do you not know the difference? Did you happen to notice this woman is wearing nursing scrubs?"

The two kidnappers looked down at Veronica's legs, below the hem of her raincoat. Then they looked at each other for answers but found none.

Grizz was the first to answer. "We were given an address and told to bring the lady back here. I don't remember nuthin' about an old woman."

"And she's wearin' a raincoat. How were we supposed to see the scrubs?" Pinky chimed in.

"You could have asked me rather than tape my mouth shut, you dolts," Veronica spat. "Winnie hasn't lived there for months now. She gifted the house to me. What do you want with her anyway?"

The voice boomed down, "THAT is none of your concern." Lowering his volume and tone, he added, "We've been given some poor intel. So now I need to decide our next move."

"I know mine," replied Veronica. "One of your goons has to take me to the bathroom, I have to pee."

"You'll just have to hold it, young lady." said the voice. "While I think."

"I can't. I need to go *now!*" Veronica answered.

"Why, because you're afraid?" said the voice, his tone mocking.

"No, you dumbass," Veronica answered. "Unlike your goons, I know the difference between an old and young woman. And one who is *pregnant.*"

The voice went silent. Pinky opened Veronica's raincoat; her baby bump evident to all three.

"Shit," whispered Pinky while Grizz stared in disbelief.

"See?" she snapped. "Pregnant. Now if you don't mind."

The old man upstairs didn't need to say a word as the two goons picked up Veronica and escorted her to the restroom, making sure they stood outside the stall, listening to her pee.

# 

Sitting in a San Diego hotel suite with a short, if not precious, lull before his next seminar, Axel Ahearne stared at the blank page on his laptop. The words just didn't want to come this morning. How had his brother made writing seem so effortless? How did Leif craft his ideas in such a way as to create one bestseller and have a second one on the way? Axel knew the partial answer to his second question because he was the catalyst for Leif's second book. Even so, it wasn't fair.

The message of finding one's path was intoxicating to his dead brother's uber fans who began calling themselves 'Leif Peepers,' in deference to his first book, *Climb Your Own Tree.* Axel thought it sounded a bit creepy, but who was he to judge those people who found inspiration in his dead brother's words?

Doing his best to keep the crowd engaged, Axel found repetition was rewarded with the unexpected: Boredom. A fact that only months ago would never have occurred to the old Axel. The risk-averse one. The straight and narrow one. The *dull* one.

Sure, as the point person for his brother's book business, he loved the attention from the fans, but lately, needed a cattle prod to keep himself motivated because of the realization Leif, and not Axel, was the main attraction. Axel was merely a placeholder and he was feeling resentment. Axel appreciated how Jules tried her best to come up with new ways to convey the same themes, but the grind of travel, performance, and second place was dragging him down.

Those feelings took a back seat once they found the new manuscript. Jules had been looking through some of Leif's belongings and accidentally came across some handwritten pages. She pieced them all together into a follow-up to *Climb Your Own Tree*.

The manuscript was a work in progress, but with a little editing by both, it was prepped and sent to the publisher who immediately set the publication in motion.

The title of this new book was *Add More Leaves*, a tome about developing multiple revenue streams. The premise stated if one stream of money stopped, like the loss of a job or a contract with a client, you still had other streams to carry you through while you sought a replacement for the recently dried-up revenue. The more streams, the healthier your business.

Axel found he had been re-energized with the potential to take the stage with new material and vigor in communicating Leif's vision that people not only could but should control their financial fate. But the thrill did not last long.

Leif's message was so clear to Axel, that he decided to act on the advice by writing his own book to add a second revenue stream to his own financial landscape. He felt this would be the bridge towards credibility of his own, rather than his present role as Leif's mouthpiece.

Playing second fiddle was almost as exhausting as keeping his brother's legacy alive. And more painful to the ego.

Axel began to put his thoughts down. He had a half-completed manuscript, so he sent a synopsis to their publisher. It was rejected. The publishing company didn't want new material from Axel, but new ideas from *Leif.* Try as they might to find any more material, he and Jules came up empty-handed.

Leif had lived long enough to publish one book and work on a follow-up. His death, not the lack of ideas, ended his literary career. The publisher floated an idea for Axel to ghostwrite another book and attach Leif's name to it. So far, Axel had deflected that idea. If he was going to write, it would be his name on the cover. Not his brother's.

"Maybe you're writing the wrong thing," Jules prompted him, carefully choosing her words.

"What do you mean?" Axel snapped, frustrated at the lack of words he desperately sought.

"Easy, tiger," she began, hoping to avoid a tiff. "All I'm saying is that maybe, writing about self-help and finding your purpose in life was Leif's thing. Maybe yours is something completely different."

"No, it's what we do. We run seminars to help people find their true purpose. We sell books to a built-in audience. It's what makes us money."

"I know," she responded. "But we have that down pat. It's not going to last forever. In the meantime, why not continue what we're doing with Leif's material, and then you can find something else to write about? Your own tree, so to speak. Think about it as insurance once Leif's fame runs out."

"Don't say that." Axel frowned. Even though he felt unfulfilled, he didn't want Leif's legacy to end. *To no longer have the last word.* Leif's fame was their only major revenue stream to date and the thought of it running dry scared him. He didn't want to admit it, but as he mulled it over, Jules did have a valid point. What would happen if this stream of money dried up before he had a chance to add a second? Then what would they do? Get jobs again? His small stipend from the Benton estate was more of a trickle, not nearly enough to cover their bills. Their publisher would move on, looking for the next author to exploit.

Axel couldn't stomach the thought of sitting behind a desk again. Building a second stream as an insurance policy was a sound idea. In fact, flowing this next stream into a reservoir made even more sense. He just needed to make it happen. Perhaps Jules was also right about a different genre.

Looking back at the blank page, only one clear thought appeared. *Where do I start?*

⌐⌐

Hector sat behind his desk in the security office at the FALM. Will Ames sat directly across from him, his left arm draped casually over the back of the chair.

"So, Mr. Ames, you came to visit Mr. Benton. The question is, why?"

"I didn't know visiting the infirm was a crime," responded Will, his sarcasm not lost on Hector. Will leaned forward, putting his hands on the desk, and stared intently at the head of security. Hector took this as a sign of confidence. *This kid is sharp.*

Will continued, "And Mr. Ames was my father. Please call me Will. Just Will."

"Okay, Will. There is no need to get defensive," Hector said, putting his hands up while acknowledging the boy used the term *was*. Losing a parent at an early age couldn't have been easy to live with. Hector hoped at least his mother was still alive. Addressing the young man he said, "Sorry for the questions but you have to understand that Mr. Benton is not the most popular figure in town and you are the first visitor he's had since he arrived months ago. You'll have to forgive my curiosity."

Will sat back in his seat. "My apologies. Let me explain. Mr. Benton is an old friend of the family. After hearing he was here at this facility, my mom asked me to come to pay our respects. She would come herself, but her work schedule is hectic." Will paused before asking, "He's not the same man I knew as a child, is he?"

Understanding now, and thankful Will still had one remaining parent, Hector chose his words carefully. "No, I'm afraid the stroke has disabled the man. It's easy to have a short visit with someone who can't speak. And he's gotten worse. When he arrived, he could make some audible sounds. but now, the only sign he shows of any awareness is in his eyes."

Will nodded his head. "Yeah, it was a brief one-way conversation. Even so, I'd like to visit again. That is, as long as I don't get interrogated each time I do so."

Hector chuckled. "No, son, I think it's a fine thing you're doing. Even unpopular residents need interaction with others, don't you think?"

"I do," Will answered, smiling back. "I didn't see the side of him you're describing. He was always good to me and my mom. Although I must admit, we didn't see him often. But when we did…" Pausing, Will shifted gears and changed the topic, commenting, "This is a nice little town, of what I've seen of it. I'd like to stick around, but to do so would mean I'd have to find a job. Am I free to go?"

Hector nodded at the young man. "Of course, you are." He thought for a moment before asking, "A job you say? Do you have a resume? We're looking for a new orderly to help with the patients if you're interested." Hector was careful not to mention anything about the former orderly, Benny Palz, who now lay in an early grave.

"Umm, I don't have one on me but can get it to you tomorrow if you'd like."

"Any references?"

"Of course. I'll send them along with the resume."

"Tomorrow is fine," said Hector. Although he couldn't see the "other," more kindly side of Harley Benton, the confidence of this young man was apparent. And if Will Ames could stomach a few visits with the unpopular old man, perhaps he could be a valuable asset to the other residents of the FALM as well.

While Hector was speaking with Will Ames, Winnie needed to make a few more phone calls before ending her day. She picked up the phone and dialed, continuing to drum her fingers nervously on the desk. This was one call she didn't want to make, privately hoping the man she was looking for had left his office for the day. She still harbored a grudge against the police for their absence in finding the FALM killer sooner which led to the death of her grandson Leif. Had they done their job correctly, he would still be among the living. The thought of this terrible episode caused her blood pressure, and anger, to rise.

"Benton Falls Police Department," the voice answered. "How can I help you?"

"I'd like to speak with Kepner, please," said Winnie.

Gary Kepner was a detective bumped up to the higher office after the previous chief had been indicted for various misdeeds. He was also the detective in charge when her grandson was killed by a lunatic. As a religious woman, she knew there were bible verses about loving thy neighbor and forgiveness. Conveniently, she avoided the verses about also loving (and forgiving) thine enemies. *Not today.*

"One moment please," came the response. There was an audible click before Winnie heard a familiar voice. "Chief Kepner here."

She choked down her contempt before speaking, "Kepner, we have a problem. I've been trying to reach Veronica all day and her calls go right to voice mail. I'm afraid something has happened to her and I need your help." She hated asking this man for any assistance but felt at this point it was an absolute necessity.

"Hello, Winnie. First of all, it's *Chief* Kepner. Secondly, how long has it been since you last spoke with her?"

"Gary, to hell with your formality. We've been through a tough scrape together. I believe I have the right to call you by your Christian name. The real problem is my girl hasn't called me back so I also have a right to be worried." Winnie's anger at the chief accelerated. "I spoke with her yesterday, in the evening. She was supposed to take me out for dinner tonight and she hasn't shown up or called me back. Something's wrong," Winnie barked.

"Ok, ok! I get it. Did you go by her house at all?"

"No, I have a facility to run. I've been calling her cell phone all day. The house phone isn't working. Tried that as well," Winnie said.

"Did you send anyone else? Do you know if she was working at the hospital? Did you even *call* the hospital? Her supervisor?"

"No, and no!" The exasperation in her voice increased. "Why aren't you already out looking for her?" Winnie avoided the hospital question, angry at herself for not thinking of calling there. *Must be slipping.*

"Winnie, you know the rule. It has to be over twenty-four hours to report a missing person."

"Bullshit," Winnie growled. "You and I know that's a rule made up on TV and you guys use it to wait for the person to come home so you don't have to work hard. But I'm telling you, she would have called if she was going to be late. Are you going to help me or not?"

She heard Kepner's audible sigh, taking that as an indication he'd been chastised. For the first time all day, she smiled, but the small joy in his discomfort didn't last long.

"I'll tell you what I can do. I'll send an officer out to her house and see if she's there. Call the hospital again but ask for her supervisor. Then call me back." Kepner got a reply, but probably not the kind he was looking for as Winnie slammed the phone down in frustration. She then picked it up again, placing the next call to the hospital where Veronica worked as a nurse.

Winnie didn't need to ask for the supervisor because the nurse who answered the phone told her Veronica had texted in sick this morning. This was a relief for Winnie. It was logical a pregnant woman with morning sickness might want to turn her phone off and get some rest. She dialed another number. He answered after the second ring.

"Kennedy speaking."

"Mr. Kennedy, it's Winnie. Have you been by the house today? I've been trying to reach Veronica. We're supposed to have dinner tonight. She may have turned her phone off."

"Miss Winnie, there is no need for formality with me. Just Kennedy is fine."

"Mr. Kennedy, old habits die hard. Good manners shouldn't die at all." The irony of her earlier conversation with the chief of police was not lost on her, but she held Mr. Kennedy in high regard for helping save Axel from Harley Benton's plot. The police chief didn't warrant that kind of respect. "And two, I don't even know your first name." She heard Kennedy try unsuccessfully to hide a chuckle. Winnie asked, "So, have you looked in on her?"

"Miss Winnie, I stopped by at lunchtime to drop off some groceries but she would have been at work today. It's on a schedule we have taped to the refrigerator. Did you try there?"

Fear gripped Winnie as a gasp escaped. She caught her breath and responded, "She called in sick today. I just spoke to the hospital, and they confirmed it!"

The urgency in Kennedy's voice came over the phone. "Miss Winnie, her car was in the drive. I just assumed she rode to work with a fellow employee. So, you have not spoken to her at all today?"

"No, that's what I'm trying to tell you. I just called the chief of police and he gave me the twenty-four hour malarky rule. I'm telling you, something is wrong and I'm worried."

"I'll head over there right now. If she called in sick, she is probably in bed. If she's there, I'll call. If not, I'll come see you."

Winnie hung up the phone for the last time that evening. The dread had returned, swarming over her. It was amplified by something she had heard in Kennedy's voice as well. Something she was not used to. Kennedy was the epitome of calm. Not this time. The foreign tone in his voice was something else.

It was fear.

"Is he back yet?" asked Grizz softly as he sat at the table, absently shuffling a deck of playing cards before dealing. He placed the deck in the middle of the table.

"I don't know," Pinky whispered back, picking up a card and then discarding it. "I can never tell until he talks."

Grizz nodded. He was indecisive if the old man was in the building or not, either. The tinted glass on the second floor offered no clues. How the old man entered and exited the building stumped the thug. Grizz was a large man with little fear. He was used to intimidating others. But the voice coming from the speakers unsettled him. Perhaps it was the anonymity. They were hired through an associate and never went face to face with anyone else so he couldn't gauge the danger level of their present employer. It didn't matter, they had a job to do, so he pushed the unsettling thoughts from his mind and focused on what he could control. One thing he wished he had power over was the sound of saws and constant banging of the construction crew next door. It wasn't too loud but it was annoying. Fortunately, the racket was only present during daylight hours. Grizz pondered how the lack of sleep would affect his judgment during this job. *Not well, Not well at all.*

He picked up a card from the deck and threw it on the pile in disgust. "I can't catch a card to save my life," he said. The two men sat at a small card table on folding chairs. Far enough away from their captive, but close enough to keep an eye on her.

"Ah, just the one I was looking for. Gin!" shouted Pinky a little too loudly as he picked up the discard, splaying out his full hand before dropping his own discard face down. "You owe me ten bucks."

Grizz frowned at his partner. "Try and collect," he said bitterly. He hated losing, especially when money was involved. But soon enough, when they finished with this job, they'd be flush for a while until the next one came along. And hopefully, one that didn't include any construction. Or mysterious bosses.

Grizz began to shuffle the deck while Pinky looked over at their captive. "Do ya think she needs anything? I mean, look at her. She's just sitting there. Water maybe?"

"It couldn't hurt. I'll grab us some coffee and you get her some water. Then I'm gonna win my money back." Grizz pushed his chair back and headed for the kitchen set up not too far away, a small lamp resting on the counter by the fridge, the only light. The building was furnished sparingly. Along with the card table, three cots lined one wall below a row of dirty windows that ran along the roof line. The sparse daylight they once offered had turned gloomy. The bathroom was located in the back corner.

Grizz grabbed a bottle from the packs stacked against the wall and tossed it to Pinky who walked over to Veronica. He gingerly peeled back the duct tape from her mouth.

Veronica began a ferocious tirade. "You idiots! What the hell do you want with me? Kidnapping a person is a felony. Do you know how much trouble you're in!"

Pinky sighed, considering the option of replacing the tape. Instead, he took the cap off the water bottle and put it to her lips. She drank heartily and when he took the bottle away, she spat a stream of water in his face.

"Take that, you bastard! Kidnapping a pregnant woman. What the hell is wrong with you!" she said, snarling. Incensed, Pinky lifted a hand as if to strike her.

"I wouldn't do that if I were you," the voice from above threatened. The boss was back. Pinky lowered his hand but sneered at Veronica.

"My sources tell me where we can find our true target. I'm now formulating an acquisition plan," explained the voice.

"And what about her," said Grizz, setting the Styrofoam coffee cups on the table, careful to move the playing cards out of the way. "What do we do with her?"

"Boys, have you ever gone fishing?" came the reply.

Grizz and Pinky looked at each other, puzzled, before looking up to the second floor again.

"Yeah, sure," Pinky said. "Lots of times"

"Well, what is essential to catching fish?"

"A boat?" answered Grizz.

Pinky offered, "Fishing gear?"

The sigh from above was loud. "BAIT, you…Gents. You need *bait* to catch the big fish. So that's what we'll do. Use the right bait and the fish will come to us, don't you think? And it seems like we have the bait right here with us."

Both men turned back to the bait the old man referred to. Veronica wriggled in her seat. Grizz noticed for the first time since her abduction, she had nothing to say. The expression on her face said it all. Veronica looked afraid.

Grizz turned back towards the old man's voice. He was still unsettled by the construction racket but more so by the unseen old man on the second floor. But Grizz also felt there was something comforting, something stable, about a man with a plan. And this old man seemed to have a good one brewing.

# 

Arabella slipped into Benton's room. She had been coming
to visit both Mrs. Hendricks and Benton for several
months now. The latter on the sly. She hoped Mrs.
Hendricks didn't die before completing her plan. But if that
happened, she had a contingency.

"Good evening, you," she said, a playful tone emanating
from her lips. "How are we feeling?"

"Goo," Benton replied. "Weal goo."

Arabella pushed her lips to one side. "Still can't make the
hard-sounding consonants, eh? Well, no matter. You keep
ticking and I'll keep sticking." She chuckled at her wordplay
while fixing the syringe. "You know the drill." She moved the
bed sheets away from his chest while he lifted his head forward,
exposing his upper back. Then she injected him.

She hoped it wouldn't be long. Stealing this stuff was getting harder and harder. She didn't want to think about what
would happen if she got caught. Her only thoughts were of
the payoff.

"Are you still playing the mute with the staff?" she asked, as she wiped the syringe with a tissue before tossing it into the waste basket. The syringe she placed back into the case.

He nodded. "Plaa."

"Right. Part of the *plan*. Which includes Will. We're not ready to tell him everything. At least, not yet."

She had just finished putting away her medical supplies when the door opened slowly and Hector stuck his head in. "Oh," he said in surprise. "I didn't know Mr. Benton had a visitor."

"Wrong door," Arabella lied convincingly. "I came to visit Mrs. Hendricks but missed the door by one. How absent-minded of me." She got up to follow Hector out the door when she had a thought. "Say, Mr.… uh?" She nodded her head towards the old man in the bed.

"Benton," Hector replied. "Harley Benton."

Arabella said his name as though it was the first time. "Mr. *Benton* doesn't get many visitors, does he?"

Hector shook his head. "I'm afraid not. He has no relatives. Looks like you're the second one to visit him since he moved in."

"Really? Well, would it be ok for me to stop in once in a while? Mrs. Hendricks isn't much company. I could visit both at the same time." Looking over at Benton, she continued, "Would you like me to visit again?"

Benton looked at her, then over at Hector. He opened his mouth to speak but stopped himself. A nod was sufficient.

"That's very nice of you. I imagine he gets rather lonely here on the Passing Lane," Hector commented.

"Then it's settled. I'm happy to do it. Can't have residents being lonely now, can we?" Arabella said as she gave Benton a wave. "Til next time. Toodles."

Getting caught wasn't Arabella's preferred path. If her lies didn't work and it came to confrontation, the other side should watch out. Her mother had named her Arabella for a reason. It was German for Beautiful Eagle. Time had stolen most of her beauty, but it left one feature ensuring her success. Her talons. Like her quick thinking and wit, they were sharp. Very sharp.

A new visitor arrived at the FALM after hours. Dottie put her hands up to stop the man.

"Visiting hours are over with. I'm sorry." She waved a hand towards the door as if the slight movement was strong enough to push him out of the exit.

"I'm not here to see a resident. I'm here at the request of Missus Ahearne." Dottie's expression changed as she picked up the phone. She put it back onto the receiver almost immediately and looked past her visitor.

"Mr. Kennedy," said Winnie, walking towards the desk. "Welcome."

"Sorry, Miss Winnie," said Dottie, "I was just calling you."

"Not a problem, dear. I knew he was coming. I'll take it from here."

Dottie stood up and asked them both, "Can I get you a coffee or something?"

"No," Winnie said. Kennedy shook his head.

"Are you sure, it's no trouble."

"Dottie, no. We have important business to discuss, don't we, Mr. Kennedy?"

Kennedy nodded.

Dottie was about to ask once more when Winnie put a finger to her lips, silencing the receptionist. This was no time for a nosy employee.

Winnie grabbed Kennedy's arm, ushered him into her office, and pushed the door shut a little too aggressively, causing it to rattle.

"She's missing and I'm worried sick," Winnie said in a half-whisper. "She won't answer her phone."

"I spent some time going around the house and looking for clues," Kennedy offered. "I didn't find anything knocked over or broken to indicate someone had been in the house. Her car was still in the driveway so I checked there. She didn't answer your calls because that is where I found her phone."

He pulled it out of his pocket and laid it on the desk. "I checked her last call. It was yesterday afternoon. To you."

Winnie looked stricken, her fear intensifying. "She picked me up and we spent some time on her front porch. We…" Winnie stopped herself. It wasn't her place to tell others of Veronica's plan to leave town. At least not yet.

Kennedy continued, "Did she say anything concerning? In her tone of voice? Any safe words? Anything at all to indicate she was in trouble?"

Winnie thought for a second before answering. "No. We made plans to go to dinner tonight. I called this morning to confirm which restaurant and, well, you know the rest." Winnie's worry lines deepened. "My lord, you think she might have been taken?"

"I do," answered Kennedy.

"But why?" asked Winnie. "Why would anyone abduct a sweet girl like that? And pregnant no less."

Kennedy thought for a moment and asked, "Do you know if she had any enemies? Anyone she owed money to? Perhaps an old boyfriend?"

"You think she has a stalker?" Winnie asked. "It's possible. We don't know too much about her life before she moved back."

"Hold on, didn't you say she called in sick?" asked Kennedy. "The last call on her phone was from last night." He picked up the phone and showed the call log.

"She didn't call. I remember distinctly they said she *texted* in sick."

Kennedy checked Veronica's text messages, upset she didn't lock her phone. Something he'd chat with her about when they next met. He found the last text message and read: "Sorry, not coming to work. Feeling sick."

The two locked eyes with the certainty something was wrong. Very wrong. Car in the drive, phone on the ground, and Veronica nowhere to be found.

"But if it was an abduction, why her?" asked Winnie. "What would anyone want with a pregnant girl?"

"I don't know, Miss Winnie. But perhaps the abductors were after someone else."

"The only one else who spends time at my house besides Vee is you. Are you suggesting…"

"Not me, Miss Winnie. You."

"Preposterous," Winnie exclaimed. "Kidnapping an old…" she stopped cold at the thought. "You really think so?"

Kennedy shrugged his shoulders. "I really don't know what to think. None of this makes sense. The only thing that does is to find Veronica."

"Yes," Winnie said. She was thankful that Kennedy didn't finish his sentence with *before it's too late*. She couldn't bear to think of a worst-case scenario. Not now.

Winnie turned her head as a thought occurred. "Wait a second, you said *find* her?" she asked, her eyes wide with hope. "Axel got her one of those thingies for your lost keys or luggage."

"They're called Key Identification Tags or KIT for short. And yes, she does have one, a Tag-It!" he said.

"Can we track it?" asked Winnie, enthusiastically.

"Yes, but it won't do us any good," he responded, taking Veronica's keys from his pocket and laying them next to the phone. "I found these next to her phone in the drive. This," he said, pointing to the phone, "tracks this." His finger moved over to the key ring.

The KIT was still attached.

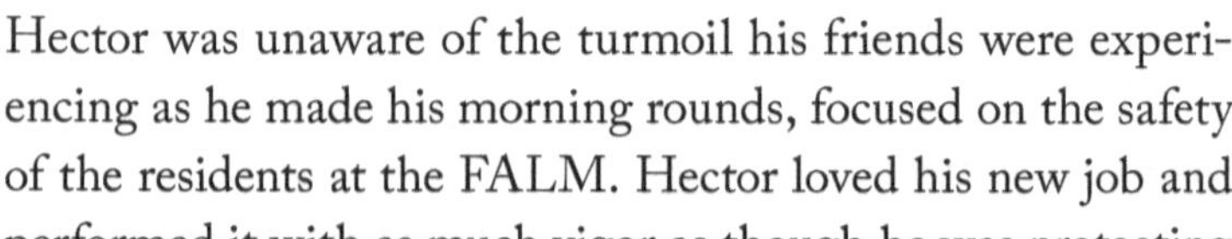

Hector was unaware of the turmoil his friends were experiencing as he made his morning rounds, focused on the safety of the residents at the FALM. Hector loved his new job and performed it with as much vigor as though he was protecting the president of the United States.

Some people who assume a position of power let it go to their heads. New bosses bully those who were once contemporaries. A police officer may garner increased ego behind the badge. Some people change with their newfound responsibilities. Not Hector. If anything, he would go out of his way to show the residents of the FALM that he was humbled and grateful to move up the ladder. That he wouldn't let the job or its duties alter his personality. The residents loved and respected him as an orderly for the way he cared for them. This would not change no matter what position he held. His good name meant more to him than a mere title. One which could be taken away just as easily as it was awarded. Hector knew it was his duty and his alone to keep his reputation sterling.

It was not uncommon for him to walk through the dining room to chat with the residents. Trying to keep up with their active lifestyles, family, and interests was difficult, but he worked hard at it. The Passing Lane was a different matter altogether. This wing was where the elderly and infirm went to die. Some suffered from dementia and asked the same questions over and over. Ever considerate, Hector would answer their questions in the same jovial manner. It wasn't their fault their brains were failing them.

Comatose patients didn't stop Hector from talking with them. He'd tell them about their friends, his own family, and the news of the day. Most of the orderlies did the minimum work and left quickly from the rooms of these patients. Hector felt even the comatose needed interaction before their time ended. He wasn't sure they could hear him but he wasn't sure they couldn't either.

Hector had just left Mrs. Hendricks's room. The poor woman lay motionless while Hector rambled on. A religious man, Hector was averse to questioning his faith, but couldn't help but wonder why a benevolent God would allow her and others like her, to suffer. Pushing the question away, he stepped up to room one sixty-seven. This was one room he dreaded to enter, not because of the condition of the patient, but because of his identity. Harley Benton stayed in this room and he was not a very nice man. The effects of a stroke had debilitated him, but Hector believed it hadn't changed the man at all. On change, his mother would warn, "You can't change the spots on a leopard." This was one leopard with plenty of spots. All dark.

He took a deep breath, pushed open the door, and looked in. The man was sitting up and awake. Hector was now bound to enter.

"Good morning, Mr. Benton," he said, cheerfully. "And how are you today?"

Benton growled something unintelligible and Hector sensed he was in a foul mood. This made him happy because now he had an excuse to make this visit a brief one.

"Anything I can do for you today?" he asked, knowing he wouldn't get an understandable answer.

"Grbbletha," barked the old man.

"It must have been nice to have a visitor or two, eh?"

Benton looked sour.

Hector went over to the bed and made sure Benton had a blanket over him. The old man scowled at him. "Well, if there is nothing else I can do for you, I've got a lot more people to help today!" Even Benton's bad attitude could not erase the pleasant mood Hector was in.

The security chief headed for the door with a wave and a cheery, "Have a nice day!" As he entered the hallway, he could have sworn he heard Benton say something sounding like, *Bug off!*

Shaking his head, he walked down the hall. "You're hearing things, Hector," he whispered to himself. Benton hadn't spoken a single intelligible word since he arrived.

Hector walked toward his office with a smile on his face and his reputation intact, glad that the most unpleasant visit of the day was now over. Or so he thought. Will Ames stood outside his office door. "Can I come in?" asked the young man.

"Sure, I didn't expect you this early."

"I've always been a wren, not an owl," Will claimed. "I like to get a good start on the day." He handed Hector a manila envelope. Hector opened it and glanced over the resume.

"After this, I'd like to stop in and see Mr. Benton, if I could."

Hector just nodded and kept reading. When done, he peppered the boy with a few questions concerning his previous jobs. Then the last one. "Why would a young man such as yourself want to work around old people?"

Will paused and thought about his answer. "Well, one has to start somewhere. I think too many people ignore older folks. But they still have something to teach us. I really enjoyed listening to the stories my grandad used to tell me."

Hector didn't miss the keywords "liked" and "used" clueing him into the fact that Will's grandfather, like his father, was no longer among the living.

"Didn't you start out as an orderly?" Will asked.

"I did indeed," answered Hector. "But it took a while to get promoted. And the job isn't easy, you know."

"I understand. Can you tell me about some of the job duties?"

"I can do better than that," Hector replied. "You wanted to see Mr. Benton? Then let's go."

He stood up and opened the door, leading Will out into the hallway. "This way to the Passing Lane," he whispered, not wanting anyone but Will to hear. "The ward where we house the sick and dying. Mr. Benton was placed on this wing because stroke victims need constant care." He opened the door to Harley Benton's room. The old person smell mixed with medicine confronted him. He watched as Will cringed at the odor. "You get used to it," he claimed. "Or maybe not."

"Mr. Benton, I'm back! And you have a visitor!" Hector said cheerfully, as he opened the shades to let in much-needed sunshine.

Harley Benton looked skeletal. He'd only been in the Passing Lane for several months now but looked as though he'd been in a prison camp; weak, emaciated, *gaunt*.

Benton opened his eyes and Hector noticed the expression on the old man as he gazed at his visitor. *Was that recognition? Glee?* It was as if he was happy to see the young man.

Will stood next to the bed and addressed him, "Good morning, Mr. Benton. I thought I'd stop by for another visit. How're you feeling today?"

Benton shifted slightly and opened his mouth. No sounds came out. Hector felt little emotion for the man. He had done some horrible things in his day. Unforgivable things. Hector silently wished the old man a long-suffering life. Then, embarrassed by the unchristian-like thought, pushed it away.

Hector watched the young man attend to Benton and thought he might just be able to handle this job. He liked to see the young man unafraid to soothe the old man. To comfort him, much the way Hector had treated his own patients.

Benton leaned forward and coughed. Instinctively, Will grabbed a tissue and put it to the man's lips as the phlegm dribbled down the side of Benton's mouth. He wiped it away and tossed the tissue into the nearby trash basket. "There," he said. "You're all set." Hector noticed that expression again. *Familiarity.* Shaking it off, he turned his attention back to Will and marveled at how the young man didn't flinch. *Yes, he might be a good fit. I wonder how he'll react to other duties.* It didn't take long to find out.

Will looked up at Hector, his nose wrinkled. Two seconds later, Hector did the same thing. They both were reacting to the stench of Harley Benton soiling himself.

"I apologize, Will," Hector said. "I'll call one of the orderlies to come clean him up."

"Not necessary. If I'm hired, I'll have to learn how to do it anyway. No time like the present." Hector marveled at the nonchalance of the boy speaking as if he'd done this before. Perhaps with his own grandfather?

"Supplies?" asked Will, shaking Hector from his thoughts. He led the young man to the supply closet at the end of the hall. They took what was necessary and went back to Benton's room where Hector watched Will with awe. *Young people are not supposed to be in this much control. This aware.*

When Will finished, Hector commented, "Jeez, I didn't actually think you'd do it. You're hired." Hector put his hand out but immediately retracted it. As Will went to the bathroom to wash his hands, Hector turned back to Benton.

"Looks like we got us a good orderly for you," he said to the old man.

Hector saw the odd expression on the old man's face once again. Except this time, even though his lips couldn't form a smile. It seemed as if his eyes could.

Veronica was uncomfortable. She was tied up and the goons had put a sleeping mask over her eyes. She tried shaking her head to move it so she could see, but that didn't work. She remained in darkness. Evidently, they felt no need to cover her ears, she could hear the sounds of hammering and sawing noises suggesting construction of some kind.

Her thoughts floated toward her missed dinner date with Winnie and cringed. *She must be worried sick.*

"She's not the only one," she mumbled out loud.

"What?" came a response from the card table as the two goons played. "You say sumpin'?" Grizz asked.

"Just clearing my throat, is all," she answered. At least they had taken the tape off her mouth to let her breathe as long as she caused no trouble. Veronica did not want to give them any reason to put it back on. She smiled weakly in their direction but kept silent. She was scared but had to stay in control.

The men went back to their card game. Veronica went back to her thoughts. *What do they want with Winnie? Why would anyone want to kidnap her? I have to figure out a way out of here. What are their plans for me if they nab Winnie?*

Veronica's stomach churned. Partly because of her pregnancy, partly her predicament. But most of all, she was hungry. Concern covered her like a chilling frost. She shivered remembering a police TV show where a detective warned his partner, "The average kidnapping victim is usually dead forty-eight hours after the abduction, so we better hurry." *What time was it? How long had she been here? Were they considering killing her?* Like the detectives, she had to act fast.

She came up with an idea. Control of the situation was key. And she had to be in control over what happened next. What was the syndrome where the captive empathized with the captors? *Ah yes, Stockholm Syndrome.* Veronica learned about the psychological condition in a seminar on how to treat those victims who developed unhealthy attachments with their kidnappers. Perhaps she could use this syndrome to her advantage.

"Hey guys, any chance I can get something to eat? I'm starving. Then maybe a chance to lie down?" When neither man moved, she added, "Boy, being pregnant is no fun."

Pinky nodded his head towards her, but Grizz didn't move from his chair.

"C'mon," Pinky said, nodding his head a little more vigorously. It wasn't a suggestion.

"She spit on you!" Grizz complained. "I don't wanna be next."

"But it's your turn," Pinky reminded.

"Yeah, sorry about that," Veronica said softly. "It's the hormones. I won't do it again."

Grizz chewed the inside of his mouth, his eyes narrowing as he thought through the apology. She helped him along with this process by pleading sweetly. "Please?"

That moved the big man. He got up from the chair and walked over to Veronica.

"You really sorry for spitting at Pinky?" he asked.

Although she couldn't move her arms, she nodded, then moved her head in a crossway motion. "Yes, cross my heart." She smiled again to show her intentions were honorable, even though they weren't. Belief was also key. The goons had to be gullible.

Grizz looked over at Pinky, who nodded. "All right, apology accepted."

Veronica giggled at his mistake and hoped he'd see it as flirting.

Pushing the mask onto her forehead, Grizz asked, "What would you like to eat, missy?"

Veronica hated the term but she looked up and continued to smile at Grizz, feeling she was gaining control. "How about something simple," she said, not wanting to sound bossy. "You wouldn't happen to have any pistachios and mustard?"

"Ewww," said Grizz, a sour expression came across his face as he thought of the revolting combination. "I have some crackers and cheese. I'll get ya something to drink, too."

"Why thank you, young sir," she said, nodding her head. "You are a gentleman helping me in my distress."

Grizz smiled back. Gullibility was one of the traits she planned to exploit.

As he walked away, she felt the puppet strings firmly in her hands. Now the question was, what could she do with the control to escape or get rescued? Stockholm Syndrome would play a key role, but she needed more. Her next thought gave her the answer and how to use it to her advantage.

*Maybe this syndrome can run in reverse.*

# Chapter Four

The next morning, Winnie sat at her desk and tried to work. Her heart wasn't in it, preoccupied with thoughts of Veronica. She slept little, her thoughts racing all night long. *If Veronica was abducted, was she safe? Were her abductors taking care of her and her unborn child? When will they contact us with demands?*

Worry kept Winnie up most of the night. It was a malicious emotion that didn't care what time it spoke to you. During the day she could keep it mostly at bay while she worked, creeping in every so often like a cold draft. But at night, worry filled the mind with endless possibilities. None of them good. Forcing herself to focus on her work seemed to be the only remedy. At least for the short term.

Shaking her head to clear the cobwebs, she steeled her nerves, determined to accomplish two things for the time being. Banish all negative thoughts and get through some paperwork to pass the time. She picked up a requisition form from Hector. He was asking for a gadget called a Tag-it! Hector was always looking for the next high-tech item to add to the security of the FALM. Winnie granted the ones making sense but some she didn't understand and therefore denied. This Tag-It! gadget was supposed to help you find things like a lost wallet, luggage, or your keys. One similar to the KIT attached to Veronica's keys. *A lot of good that did.*

Keeping up with the amount of paperwork this business generated as well as the rules and regulations was one thing. Adding technical jargon and equipment one didn't understand was quite another. *How was an old lady like me able to keep up?*

Winnie shook her head. Hector was constantly misplacing his keys. You'd think her head of security would have enough sense to keep those items on his person at all times. The irony seemed to be lost on the man. The fun part was catching him without his keys and asking him to unlock a door. She didn't care about what was on the other side, she just got a kick out of watching him squirm.

Well, if this item helped him be better at his job, so be it. She truly cared for the young man and wanted to ensure his success. She decided if he lost his keys a lot, he might lose this gadget as well. She changed the '1' to a '3' deciding to keep two in her desk in case he misplaced the first and keep one for herself. Looking once again at her watch before signing the requisition form, she was ready to move on to her next chore.

She propped up her sleep-deprived head with her chin in hand, resting the elbow on the desk, as she contemplated her next task. *It's going to be a long day.* Slowly, she picked up the phone and dialed.

"Detective?" she said, once Chief Kepner picked up. "Your twenty-four hours are up. You need to go over to Veronica's house."

Gary Kepner sighed. "Miss Winnie, the title is *Chief* Kepner. I've been the police chief since earlier this year."

"Jesus, Mary, and Joseph, and all the bald-headed angels," Winnie responded, her disrespect for the officer evident. She continued, "What I need is for someone to go over and investigate her disappearance. There must be evidence to show she was taken." Winnie avoided mentioning the phone or car keys. Last night she had instructed Kennedy to return to the house and put the items on the counter where a police search would confiscate them, telling the ex-butler the police wouldn't blame him for moving the evidence out of the rain. He was part of Veronica's household and at the time had not yet determined she was missing.

"Have you interviewed anyone yet?" Winnie asked. "Talked with the neighbors? Done anything??"

"Miss Winnie," the chief began, "We're just starting the investigation in the…um…disappearance of Veronica. I can't go into details, but I also don't appreciate one of your people asking around the neighborhood. Interfering with an ongoing investigation is a crime, you know."

Winnie winced at the veiled reference that she had begun the investigation herself with the help of Kennedy. The threat, she chose to ignore.

A Beatitude popped into her head. *"Blessed are those who mourn, for they shall be comforted."* Although Winnie continued to mourn the loss of her grandson, there would be no comfort should she need to mourn for Veronica and her unborn child, *Leif's child.* The only part of him left.

Deciding to go on the offensive rather than defend herself, she spat, "If'n you'd do your job, we wouldn't have to do it for you!"

"LET US…" Kepner began but softened his tone. "Please, let us do our job." Kepner paused before starting again, "Look, Miss Winnie, we're going by the book on this. I know it's frustrating but you have to let the professionals handle this. We're going to find her, OK?"

Winnie knew she wasn't the only one upset about Veronica's disappearance. She could tell it weighed heavily on the chief's mind as well by the way he barked at her. *He's agitated. Serves him right.*

"Have you been contacted by anyone? If this was a kidnapping, there would be a demand. Have there been any? A phone call? A ransom note?"

"Don't you think if we had anything, you'd be the first to know?" Winnie's frustration surfaced. What kind of kidnappers were these people? What did they want and how come they haven't reached out? Fear crept in. Lack of knowledge opened the door to speculation. Speculation led to endless possibilities. All of them negative.

"Winnie, we have all our resources on this case. Again, let us handle this."

"All right then, do your job. But keep me in the loop on any developments, will you?"

Winnie heard the chief sigh, probably because he knew her reputation. Hanging up the phone, she was convinced she'd finally pushed the chief to act. They would investigate their way but she was damned if she'd sit idly on the sidelines. Winnie was a woman used to giving orders and taking action. And getting her way. She was too old now to be chided or threatened by the likes of Kepner. He could bark all he wanted. Winnie knew one thing the chief had yet to learn. He may possess a loud bark, but it was no match for Winnie. She had something he didn't.

A vicious bite. And when she chomped onto something, she didn't let go.

Winnie went back to work to occupy her mind. She had fallen behind and needed to catch up, but it was difficult given the circumstances. She didn't get far when Dottie interrupted on the intercom. "Miss Winnie, Mr. Kennedy is on line one."

Winnie hit the button as she drew the phone to her ear. "Mister Kennedy, any news?" she asked, excitedly.

"I'm afraid not," he responded. "I've been through the whole house and haven't found anything. Not even evidence of a struggle."

"Have you checked the answering machine?" she asked.

"Miss Winnie, Veronica threw that relic out the day she moved in. And had the landline disconnected as well. With cell phones, she didn't see the need."

Winnie sighed, knowing Veronica's cell phone was sitting on the counter in full view of Kennedy.

"What about the neighbors? Anyone hear anything?"

"Miss Winnie, I canvassed the neighborhood talking to anyone within earshot. No one heard a thing. No one saw anything. I'm sure the police will repeat this task once…*if* they come by to investigate."

Winnie felt her temperature rise. "They better, or I'll have the badge of that no account Kepner. I spoke to him a short while ago but I'll call him again soon and bug him until he takes action."

"Wait, that won't be necessary. A police cruiser just pulled up. I'll let them in and report back to you." Winnie noticed Kennedy had paused. There was good reason.

"You do know you have to inform Master Axel and Miss Jules," he said. Due to their new business arrangements, Axel had pleaded with Kennedy to drop the 'Master,' but some habits lingered.

Again, Winnie sighed. "Yes, yes, I know. I've been dreading making that call. But it must be done. Let me know what the police say. Goodbye, Mr. Kennedy."

A question hung in the air without verbalization. *How would they react to the news?*

Not well, thought Winnie, shaking her head as she dialed Axel's cell number. *Not well at all.*

Veronica also slept fitfully. Even though she had the luxury of movement, her abduction, pregnancy, and the lumpy cot on which she slept made her miserable. Still, it was more comfortable than trying to sleep sitting upright, bound, and gagged.

She had successfully negotiated her limited freedom. "I'm pregnant," she chided. "Where am I going? You think I can just waddle away?" With a promise to behave, the two kidnappers begrudgingly gave her a place to rest.

"Try and escape once, and it's back in the chair," Pinky threatened, before making hand motions she interpreted as him replacing the mask and the return of duct tape.

"Don't worry, I promise to stay put," she said, patting her stomach and wording the sentence so that she didn't say any-thing about being *rescued*. Someone had to be looking for her. Winnie and Kennedy would not let her absence go unnoticed. They'd be the first ones out in the search party. Even if they had been warned not to call the police, they'd be investigating themselves.

Although she promised not to escape, the temptation to try was strong. However, reason proved to be stronger. In the event she made it outside, waddling to freedom didn't seem like a viable option. The two thugs would have no trouble overtaking her and dragging her back. Then she was sure to lose what comfort the cot had to offer. She softly touched her chin where the tape had left a burn, solidifying her resolve to be patient. But that didn't mean she couldn't observe her surroundings. One never knew what might aid in one's rescue.

They were holding her in a concrete building with a high ceiling. The cement floor was a cold gray, the walls painted a dull white. All the windows needed a good cleaning, Thin enough to let in light, and high enough to keep prying eyes out. Or reach. She couldn't expect to get anyone's attention there.

At either end there were doors, but again, her condition wouldn't allow her to get far. Boxes and equipment were strewn along the sides and corners of the building. A lone extending pole with a sponge on the tip stood in the far corner. A solitary sentry awaiting duty to reach the dirty windows for cleaning. She surmised this place was used for storage. Smart. Little to no traffic and construction noises to drown out screams for help. A perfect place to hide a kidnapping victim.

The second floor wasn't much of one. It began with metal stairs leading to a framework of metal flooring. She could see the feet of anyone walking up there through the slats in the metal. There was an office with a dark window facing the stairs, the lone structure on the framework that looked out of place.

These two goons no longer frightened her. She could see they had captured the wrong woman but also felt they wouldn't hurt her. No, these guys were just the henchman. The hired help with no decision-making capabilities.

What truly scared her was the unknown old man from the second-floor office. He'd not been back since yesterday. She wondered if he'd make an appearance today, but even more curious how he came and went unseen. If he did show up, she'd listen intently to find out any tidbit of his plan to kidnap Winnie. But she'd do so silently. It was one thing to speak with the two men who had just freed her, another to communicate with this unknown person. There was a reason he had kept his identity hidden. For her own safety, Veronica wanted no part in exposing him or understanding why he deemed his secrecy necessary.

No, she didn't believe these two goons would hurt her on their own, but what if they got orders from upstairs? What would happen next?

She didn't have to wait long to find out. The voice of the old man came from the second floor. "Gentlemen," he said, as both men scrambled to their feet and came to stand by Veronica.

"I see you've relaxed your hold on our visitor." Grizz began to explain but the old man cut him off.

"Stop. It's good to see you treating her well. Make sure she gets something to eat and drink." As an afterthought, he said, "And don't forget bathroom breaks. You know how pregnant women get when it comes to that."

The man upstairs took on a menacing tone, contradicting his previous one, "Let's be clear. If she's to be free of her restraints, then make sure she causes no unnecessary trouble. Freedom comes with a cost, does it not?"

Veronica felt a chill up her spine.

"Yessir," both men said in unison.

"Pinky, could you step up here please?"

Pinky looked forlornly at Grizz as if the task was equal to taking out a smelly bag of trash. The smaller man hesitated. Veronica took this to mean she wasn't the only one wary of the old man.

"*Now*, please!" came the order from upstairs prompting Pinky to rush up the steps.

"It's time for phase two of our operation. We have to follow up with our ransom note. Did you leave it in a place they'd find it as requested?" Pinky shuffled his feet before turning to his partner in crime. "Grizz?" he said, his eyes pleading.

Grizz smiled, evidently proud of himself. "I put it where only one person could find it. If the police got involved, I didn't want them getting ahead of themselves. You know, slow 'em down."

"And who would that person be?" asked the boss.

"The one who plays the piano. I stuck it in between the pages of the sheet music, smart, eh?"

The boss let out an audible sigh. "Miss Veronica," he began. "Who in your home plays the piano?"

Veronica answered slowly, "I do."

"Anyone else, dear?"

"No. Just me."

Pinky slapped a hand against his forehead. Grizz looked confused.

There was another pause before the old man spoke once more. "Very well. I have a task for you to accomplish. We'll have to improvise. If the fish won't come to the bait, we'll just have to retrieve the fish ourselves. We have to wait until the time is right. Do *not* make a move until I tell you. The directions are in here."

An envelope slipped under the door and Pinky picked it up.

"And gentlemen?" he added, the menacing tone had resurfaced. "Don't let me down again."

Pinky went down the stairs while reading the printed note. He handed it to Grizz who read it and nodded in agreement.

"We have a package to pick up," Pinky whispered, a sly grin appearing.

The old man was adamant. "Again, not until I give the order. We have to make sure the timing is right. Understood?"

Both men nodded.

The talk of retrieving fish and how Pinky pronounced 'package' raised the alarm for Veronica. The terms 'package' and 'fish' could mean a series of items. Most likely a person. She surmised the two were not going to the post office or market but to a certain assisted living facility. Veronica felt a wave of helplessness at the thought. How could she get the word out to warn Winnie? The answer was clear… and frightening. She couldn't. But maybe she could stall them by sending them on a mission. "Psst," she whispered to Grizz. "Do you think you could go to the store and get me some pistachios and mustard, please? I have a terrible craving."

Grizz winced at the thought of the vile combination. "But why? Are you the kind of person who also dips their french fries in mayonnaise?"

She nodded and giggled, wiggling a finger that said, 'Come here.' He got closer as she whispered the specific brands she preferred. It wasn't so much a preference as it was a distraction. The longer she kept the goons from Winnie, the better.

"Because it's salty and spicy, like me," she said, a grin plastered on her face, her Stockholm Syndrome plan at work.

Grizz winced and shook his head in disgust. He looked up at the office for permission. "Can we?" When no answer returned, he told Veronica, "Sure, we can do that."

"I'm goin' too," Pinky yelled up to the office. Again, no answer, meaning the boss had already left.

Grizz let his shoulders slump. "Sorry Vee, we have to…" He walked her to the chair and tied her loosely. He did not place either the mask or the duct tape on her. This was a good sign her plan was producing results. Build trust to gain freedom and aid in her escape. *Baby steps.*

"Behave yourself, missy," Grizz whispered.

She replied, "Scouts honor. I promise." Then winked at him for good measure.

After the two left on their errand, Veronica studied the row of windows. The subdued light of morning found its way into the building casting dark shadows underneath. Soon she would hear the sounds of construction begin. Dark thoughts began to creep in, *When will they go after Winnie? What if her ploy didn't help? What would happen once they didn't need either of them?*

Then a ray of hope appeared as she formulated an idea. She needed to come up with a sign that would alert someone of her presence, yet not make it obvious she was crying for help from her captors if they saw it. If they did, she needed culpable deniability. Her gaze went around the building again, resting on the extendable cleaning pole in the corner. Looking back at the windows, she realized she didn't have to look out.

She only needed someone else to look in.

⁓

"Axel," began Theodore 'Ted' Holcomb, Leif's publisher. "We have a Golden Goose here and what you want to do will kill it before it's time." Axel Ahearne ran a hand through his hair as he listened. He had promised to keep his brother's name alive by roaming the country delivering seminars and speaking to Leif's fans about climbing their own trees. And of course, the golden egg, selling his books. It was a profitable venture for both publisher and speaker, but Axel was tired of the constant drudgery of travel. Of sleeping in hotel rooms and not his own bed.

Axel kept his brother close by having a portion of his ashes mixed with carbon fiber made into a ring. He wore it on his right hand at all times, including on stage, feeling that if it weren't for his brother, Axel wouldn't be where he was and felt Leif deserved a place on stage just as much, if not more, than Axel himself. When he felt nervous or anxious, Axel would twirl the ring around his finger. Talking to his publisher, he found himself doing so now.

"Son, look, you did a decent job with the second book," said the publisher. "So what if no one knows? But Leif is the brand we're selling and you need to help me. Your seminars are the engine driving book sales and without you and Jules, that goose is dead in the water."

Axel heard Winnie's voice in his head. *What happened to the promise you made of keeping your dead brother's name alive?*

*Of his always having a last word?* She had a point. On one hand, he felt guilty even thinking about what he was asking. His brother had died protecting Winnie but had left a legacy of sorts. One extremely popular book and a second with the potential to outsell the first. On the other hand, if Leif's novel, *Climb Your Own Tree*, resonated with anyone, it would be Axel and his desire to shift gears and make a name for himself.

Axel pondered what to say next. He didn't like the idea of killing off Leif's brand but the itch to write his own material was strong. "Ted, I've got another idea you may like. It's general fiction about…"

Ted cut him off. "I get it, everyone wants to write, but you have to understand, this is a tough business. Do you know how many books are published each year that rarely get read let alone sold? Especially now with the ease of self-publishing? We can only represent so many titles per year and have to make sure our choices sell." The publisher paused for a moment and then added. "I'm fighting for my life here. I need you guys to keep Leif's brand going. If you can find any more notes or even if you come up with another idea similar to Leif's let's work on that and keep this gravy train running. The marketing team has leaked there may be more text out there and we can use that to our advantage. His fans don't need to know he didn't pen it. You could be his ghostwriter. We could make this gravy train run for another few years. Whaddya say?"

"Theodore, listen to me." Axel used the proper name when agitated. "I'm not ready to commit to deception," he said, dodging the idea. "But I can start pitching the new book. And if I do this for you, you need to promise me you'll take *my* work seriously, OK? This train, as you call it, won't last forever. I need a guarantee you'll work with me to build my own brand before that happens, Understand?"

"Sure, kid. I understand. But remember, this is a tough business and you never know what will sell and what won't. There are no guarantees."

Axel shook his head. He knew eventually Ted's euphemisms of a gravy train would get derailed and the golden goose would stop laying eggs. He wanted to do whatever he could to build his brand before those inevitabilities. He had a lot of decisions to make. One of them included thinking it may be time to replace the train conductor himself.

Axel didn't have time to mull that thought very long. Interrupted by his cell phone, he saw it was Winnie.

"Ted, I gotta take this call. It's my grandmother. We're not through with this discussion." Before his publisher could respond, Axel hung up and connected with Winnie.

"What's up?" he asked cheerfully. The emotion didn't last long as Winnie filled him in on what had occurred in Benton Falls. Winnie was right about telling Axel about Veronica's disappearance. He didn't take it well at all.

In an effort to take her mind off her troubles, Winnie decided to go shopping. In her mind, optimism and pessimism had attacked each other relentlessly. She felt there was no room for pessimism because the pain would be too great. But dark thoughts continued to creep in no matter how many times she tried to banish them. Aiding the positive side, Winnie decided to buy a little gift for Veronica for *when,* not if, she returned.

The grocery store was crowded. A development Winnie had tried to avoid because she hated crowds. In an attempt to minimize her exposure to congested aisles and long waits at the checkout line, she arrived at the store early. The ploy had failed miserably as there were shoppers everywhere.

The old cliché for a pregnant woman was the appetite for the pickle and ice cream combination. Not Veronica. She had a mind and uterus of her own when it came to craving, her selection odd. Winnie had heard of some strange cravings before. Ice, rubber, chalk, toothpaste, and even ashes. Weird food combinations like sardines with ketchup and peanut butter and marshmallows. At least Vee's cravings contained actual food, despite the strange combination of pouring de-shelled pistachios into a bowl and covering them with a spicy mustard. She would then devour the concoction with a spoon as if eating a bowl of breakfast cereal. Winnie was aware not just any brand would do. And the specific brands she sought were sold only at a few places. This store happened to be one of them.

As Winnie turned down the aisle to look for the mustard before heading to find the pistachios, she overheard two men speaking loudly in the next aisle over.

When she heard the first one say, "I don't think that's the right mustard," she turned her head toward the conversation. When the second responded, "Mustard is mustard. If she doesn't like it, she can lump it. We don't have time for this. Now, where are the pistachios?" her ears perked up.

The first one countered, "Look, the girl is pregnant and under some pressure. The least we can do is get her the brand she wants. It's supposed to be spicy."

Fully engaged in their conversation, Winnie raised her eyebrows in surprise. Pregnant? Similar cravings as Veronica? She had never heard of another craving such as this before, yet here it was. *This sure is a small world.*

The thought of Veronica being held against her will with whatever demons had abducted her, made Winnie catch her breath. She fought back the urge to cry, allowing only a single tear to escape before wiping it away with her index finger.

"She said salty and spicy, like her," pleaded the first man. "Salty and spicy."

Winnie let out a small laugh. *Sounds just like something Veronica would say. That poor husband.*

"Well, send another bullet and kill poor buck," the second man replied, the frustration in his voice apparent. "Let's just get the nuts and go, can we?"

Winnie shook her head at the absurd saying, as she grabbed the bottle of mustard from the shelf and began to push her cart forward, unaware of the irony of using odd sayings herself. She stopped, deciding to get another bottle of mustard and then grab two bags of pistachios.

*Have to remain optimistic.* She'd give one set to Veronica and keep one at the FALM for when Veronica would visit. *Never know when a craving will strike. Salty and spicy, just like her.*

Curious, she went into the next aisle looking to share her experience with the husband and his friend, wanting to ask where he came up with the odd saying but when she turned into the aisle, both men had already left.

Shaking her head at the whole episode, Winnie found the pistachios and with her optimism winning over, headed for the check-out counter. "Men," she whispered. "Send another bullet and kill poor buck. What a ridiculous saying."

With guys like those two, women and bucks were not safe, she thought. *Mainly from their lack of empathy. And their absurdity.*

Hector was relieved. Will Ames was working out better than the head of security had planned. The young man was smart, empathetic, and seemed to anticipate issues from the residents without complaints or drama. These were the good qualities he and the FALM looked for in their orderlies. Under Harley Benton's watch, hiring anyone off the street for little pay was the norm. But then so was the end result. The old adage of 'you get what you pay for' couldn't have been more accurate. Himself excluded, of course.

Winnie had instituted strict hiring guidelines and Will was the perfect fit for the FALM, the Center's good fortune he'd signed on. Unlike the bully, Benny Palz. That punk had a mean streak and looked for trouble every chance he got, especially his run-ins with Hector, whom he had vindictively labeled, Ratboy. Hector cringed at the image of the man and began to think how glad he was his adversary was dead, having succumbed to a drug overdose. Hector pushed the thought away. His parents and religion taught one shouldn't speak ill of the dead. No matter how miserable they were in life.

Young orderly Ames was different. He even excelled in his interactions with the residents. Hector had the same quality and marveled at how the residents took to Will as if he were a nephew or grandson.

Hector looked on in admiration as Will walked through the dining room at lunchtime. His attention to the residents was well received. A joke told to the gents at one table elicited laughter. Flirting with the ladies eating their dessert prompted blushes and girlish giggling.

Will stopped at Mrs. Augustine's table and moved her water glass closer so she could reach it. She had just taken a mouthful of meat and looked up in appreciation. A quizzical look came over her face. Her head began to jerk forward and hands instinctively reached for her throat.

Hector recognized it immediately. "Choking!" he yelled, then began to run towards the table but Will had already lifted the old woman, his arms underneath hers, his fist pressed just under her bosom. He began to deliver the Heimlich maneuver.

Hector looked on helplessly as Will continued to push. The other residents stopped their discussions or meals and watched with trepidation to see if the young man could save the elderly woman from choking to death. It didn't take long. With one final push, Mrs. Augustine hacked up the piece of meat. It sat on her lip while Will placed her gently onto the chair. He grabbed a napkin and covered the choking hazard before lifting it away from her. He then brought her water glass to her lips while commenting, "You're fine now, drink."

The residents cheered Will's success causing Hector to look around the room. It seemed everyone had joined in. Except Will, who, despite all the noise, focused solely on poor Mrs. Augustine, still shaking from the ordeal.

Hector marveled at the young man's ability to assess the situation, take action, and then comfort. Once he felt confident the crisis was averted and the dining room settled back into normalcy, Hector walked to Winnie's office to inform her of the incident and the brave actions of young Will. When he returned to the dining room, Will was still sitting next to Mrs. Augustine, a hand placed softly against her back in comfort.

Walking back to his office, he found himself smiling. "He's definitely a keeper," Hector whispered to himself as he opened his office door and walked in.

Chief of Police Kepner sat at his desk, head in hand. The investigation was going nowhere and he was feeling the heat. He was especially tired of hearing from the Ahearne woman. The old lady was relentless in her quest to find the missing pregnant girl. A lot of people in these situations either let the police do their job or fade away after the initial frustration. Not Winnie Ahearne. She was like a pit bull, her teeth firmly attached to his leg with no hope of breaking free.

His detectives had been meticulous. Going over the crime scene, interviewing multiple people, and doing a thorough job of attempting to piece together a puzzle that seemed unsolvable. They didn't even find a ransom note, so how could they find a perp if the perp wasn't demanding anything?

Chief Kepner toyed with the theory the young woman may have just left everything behind and fled. He could see why she might want to start a new life, an attempt to run away from the horrific death of her fiancé. Hell, he'd even given it thought himself. Moving to a new location where no one knew him. The prospect of a new beginning, a new *life*, appealed to him. No one would blame either of them.

He shook the thought away. There were too many clues leading to abduction to support the runaway theory: The car was still in the driveway, no clothes had been taken, and the empty suitcases were stashed in a hall closet. Credit and debit cards went unused and her cell phone was found sitting on the counter. It was as if she had just disappeared. *An alien abduction?* He shook his head at such an absurd thought. No, the clues led to an earthly one and he was going to find the perp. And the girl.

People went missing every day and a fair number of those cases were never solved. Kepner vowed the Bucholz woman would not be one of those cases. But he needed help. Someone just as hard-nosed and ferocious as Winnie Ahearne. He didn't need an old lady with the jaws of a pit bull. Just the next best thing. Someone the chief could trust to uncover every clue. Someone who wouldn't be afraid to bend the rules. Or break one or two.

The chief picked up his phone and dialed. After three rings, the voice on the other side barked, "Nick Holmes."

"Nick, I need you in my office, pronto." The chief had called the Bulldog.

After the choking incident, Will made his way to Benton's room. Will recalled his first visit. It was one-sided as the old man lay motionless in his hospital bed. His second visit was more intimate, if not embarrassing. This visit would be different. As he entered Benton's room, he was greeted with a partial smile, causing Will to return his own. It was amazing to Will how two people could bond over the act of cleansing another's defecation. Embarrassing or not.

What he hid was the pity he felt for the old man. Who would want to be in that kind of condition? A stroke incapacitated the man who had everything going for him. Money, a large manor, a town named after him…and power. *None of these could matter to the old man now.*

A strange recollection appeared from a high school history lesson of King Richard yelling from the battlefield, "My kingdom for a horse!" The old man would probably give up his vast fortune for something more valuable. Youth.

"How we doing today?" he asked, cheerfully. Benton rewarded him with a weak thumbs up from his right hand. Then the old man offered another gesture; a forefinger touching his thumb while the other three fingers splayed outward, his hand trembling back and forth.

"Things are OK?" Will asked, misinterpreting the sign. Benton grunted, bent his hand downward, and swirled the fingers in a circular motion. They weren't trembling. They mimicked writing. "Oh, you want to write something?"

The old man nodded.

"Hold on. I'll be right back." Will left the room and shortly returned with a pad and a pen, handing both to Benton. *So, the old man could write.* Will knew the man understood what he was saying, but the stroke had caused enough damage so he couldn't communicate back. Or so Will thought. *Has the old man been playing possum?* Benton scratched out a note and turned the pad over so the young man could read.

Help was the first word. The letters were childlike but Will could still understand.

"Of course," Will assured him. "I'll help any way I can."

The old man lifted his right hand still in its writing pose. This time he *did* mean, 'OK.'

Benton went back to the pad. The second word was Trust? Will nodded. "Yes, you can trust me."

Again, Benton raised the okay sign.

The writing continued. The word Mother came next. Benton had underlined it. Benton's mother had to be long dead. Then it hit him. "You want me to call *my* mother?" he asked, confused. The old man shook his head no. He opened his mouth to speak but closed it before anything came out. Frustrated, he wrote again. Message.

Will asked the question, "Do you want me to get a message to my mother?"

Benton nodded.

*Why does he want to get a message to her? To thank her? Or does he need something he can't get here?* Will was still confused but chose not to show it. Placating the old man, he replied, "Sure. I can do that."

Benton flipped the page and began writing again. This time it didn't appear to be just one word but a longer message. Intended for Will's mother.

It was his mother who had sent him on the first visit. Once he told her of the old man's condition, she insisted he continue to visit. She was pleased when he told her he'd landed the orderly job. And now, Mr. Benton had gone from comatose to communicating. It was all so mysterious. Yet, encouraging. *Have I had some influence on Mr. Benton's recovery? Does he want to thank her for sending me?*

When finished, Benton folded up the piece of paper and handed it to Will, who put it in his shirt pocket.

The old man wrote another word on the first page with all the other ones. It was Discreet. To illustrate his discretion, Will took the pad from the old man and ripped the filled page from it. Despite his confusion, he tore the page up and placed the pieces in his pants pocket for disposal later. Will then put the pad and pen in the nightstand drawer next to the bed before lifting a finger to his lips. Discretion adding another layer to the bond they were building.

Axel and Jules rushed into Winnie's office, followed by Dottie, who was panting. "They ran right by me. I'm so sorry Miss Winnie."

Winnie shook her head. "No worries, Dottie. This is my grandson, Axel, and his girlfriend Jules. They just came in from California. Kids, this is my new receptionist, Dottie."

Winnie dipped her head and looked over her glasses at Axel before asking, "She *is* still your girlfriend, isn't she?"

Axel nodded, then shot a glance at Dottie. Winnie picked up on the cue. "Dottie, be a dear and please bring some coffee for my guests, okay?"

Axel waited for the receptionist to leave before attacking his grandmother with questions.

"What's the latest? Do you have any clues? Why would someone do this? Tell us everything!"

Winnie looked sternly at her grandson. "I will, but first, sit down and compose yourself. This is a retirement home, not a smarmy reality TV show!"

Axel took a breath at the scolding. Chastened, he whispered, "Sorry."

"Now," Winnie began, "We don't know too much. Kennedy and I believe she was abducted in her driveway just as she was leaving for work. We don't know why or who but Kennedy doesn't think she was the actual target."

"Wait, what?" Axel had a confused look on his face. Jules jumped in.

"So, someone else was the supposed target? Are you thinking it was you?" she asked, pointing to Winnie. "Because it was your house?"

"Yes. The deed hasn't been transferred yet. It's still in my name. I sure wish they had snatched me instead of Veronica, I would have given them a licking they would not soon forget. Picking on a poor pregnant woman is a dastardly act."

Axel and Jules looked at each other in surprise. Only one person in the room missed the irony of an old woman seeing herself as a harder target to capture than a woman half her age, despite being visibly pregnant.

"What does Kennedy say?" Axel asked.

"We've discussed it and he thinks it's one possibility that it was me they were after, but for the love of Pete, we don't know why. The police are thinking it has to do with money. It's what most kidnappers want."

"But you don't have a lot of money and Leif didn't leave a large amount to Veronica either. It's not like she has millions," Axel said, with the authority of one who knew the finances of his brother's estate.

"Have you received a ransom note yet?" asked Jules. "A phone call? Any communication at all?"

"No, nothing yet, which is also surprising. Until you buy into the theory I was the target and not Veronica." Winnie said. "Once they found this out, the kidnappers would have to regroup and find me. Maybe that's why we've heard nothing."

"But why?" Axel asked. "Why would anyone want to kidnap you?"

"That's the million-dollar question, boyo," she answered. "If I knew the answer, we'd be on our way to solving this mess."

Axel shook his head in disbelief. "Why do bad things happen to us? We're good people, right? I don't understand why God lets bad things happen to good people."

Winnie cleared her throat. "He doesn't. We were all born with free choice. You can't have free choice *and* interference at the same time. God lets the bad actors make wrong decisions and watches as it plays out, dealing with them later."

"Good point, but let's get back to the details we now know," Jules said, trying to take control.

Axel interrupted her, his alpha male emerging, "I got this." Winnie noticed as Jules stopped and looked at the floor in deference.

"One," he began, "Harley Benton is incapacitated which rules him out as a suspect."

"Two, he has no heirs looking for revenge or the return of his estate."

"Three, Winnie has no other enemies we can think of."

"Not that we can *think* of," Jules chimed in.

"That's right, Who have you pissed off lately, woman?" Axel's attempt at humor fell flat as both women glared at his insensitivity.

Jules broke the uncomfortable silence. "Unless they want you to get to someone else?"

"Who?" Axel asked.

"You and Kennedy."

"What? Ridiculous!" Axel barked at her. "It doesn't make sense. Why would anyone want us?"

Jules bit the inside of her cheek before answering, "It's merely a theory."

Winnie rubbed an eyebrow as if a headache was oncoming. "And it does make sense. Axel, think about it. What do you and Kennedy have in common?" He looked perplexed so Winnie added, "Wait for it..."

Recognition appeared on Axel's face. "Control of Harley Benton's estate," he said.

"There it is," said Jules, smiling that her 'theory' had legs.

"Took him long enough," complained Winnie.

"But that still doesn't make sense to me. Benton can't be behind this. He can't even communicate."

"But perhaps Harley Benton's *enemies* can," reasoned Jules, her point causing another silence in the room.

A knock on the door startled everyone as Kennedy poked his head in before entering the room. He took off his raincoat but left his gloves on. Addressing the couple, he said, "Hey folks, glad you're here." Then added, "But not under these circumstances."

"So, you think the kidnappers were after Winnie, too?" asked Jules.

"Yes, I'm absolutely sure of it. More than ever now."

"What makes you say that?" asked Axel.

"Because while the police were searching in all the wrong places, I looked in one right place. I checked the music book on the piano in the parlor. Inside was the ransom note," Kennedy explained, as he pulled the envelope containing the kidnapper's demands from his raincoat pocket and waved it at the stunned group.

# Chapter Six

Veronica sat on the bed munching her concoction of pistachios and mustard. It wasn't the mustard she normally used but would suffice, grateful she got anything at all. She took another spoonful as she watched the two thugs play a hand of gin rummy.

"Ha," yelled Pinky, laying his cards down on the table. Grizz scowled as he wrote the final score on a notepad and set up the next game. He wore the look of a man who wanted to do more than stare. Veronica paused to think of what the hulk of a man with a mean streak could do to a person. Or already had. She didn't want to find out so she decided it was time to get closer to these two.

"Hey guys," she said, pointing her spoon at the men. "Can I show you how it's done? I'm bored just sitting here."

"If you're bored, you could do the dishes," offered Pinky.

"Hey!" Grizz barked, "That's not nice. Where are your manners?"

"It's okay guys, I planned on doing them anyway if you'd let me. Another thing. Those windows need to be cleaned. They are filthy." Veronica pointed upward. "And disgusting."

Both men eyed her suspiciously. She tried to set their minds at ease. "What, you think I can climb up there and escape through one of those windows? Seriously?"

When she saw the look between the two as they realized the absurdity of *that* escape plan, she continued, "I just can't stand looking at the filth. I promise if you let me play a few hands, little Miss Suzie homemaker here will have this place spotless in no time."

Grizz scrunched his mouth before saying, "Okay, but no funny stuff." And to the smaller man, he barked, "Get her a chair, will ya? Jeesh, no manners at all."

"Why me? Why don't you do it, Miss Manners?" Pinky complained.

"One, you're closer. And two…" Grizz leaned in, his upper body covering half the table. "Ya might want to be careful with the remarks. I got nuthin' to lose except at cards. Everything else is on the table."

Veronica recognized the veiled threat. So did Pinky as he frowned but rose and found another chair. Sensing they both thought she was an easy target at cards, Veronica put a hand to her mouth and coughed to hide a smirk. *Let them think what they want.*

"Remind me of the rules again?" she asked, feigning ignorance.

"Only if you put that bowl in the sink and clean it now. The smell is nauseating." Pinky held his nose to illustrate his point as Veronica did as she was told before returning to the table.

Once she felt their explanation of the game boosted the belief of their superiority, she barked at Pinky, "C'mon and deal already." Then she smiled coyly at Grizz. *Did he just blush?*

She allowed a loss in the first game, listening intently to get any information she could playing the hapless female role to a tee. An attempt to disarm the brutes so she could discover key facts which could aid in her rescue. Even though he lost again, Grizz appeared to take solace in the fact he was beaten by a man and not a girl. Especially a pregnant one. She began her line of questioning simply enough. "Why is it you tough guys always have nicknames?" she asked with an air of innocence. Part of her Stockholm Syndrome strategy was to divide and conquer, then act as peacemaker. The divide part meant she had to 'poke the bear.' Cause friction between the two men. The tinder was already present. She just needed a match.

"I got mine 'cause back in my hometown I was bigger than most of the kids growin' up. And with the blond hair and all, I looked like a grizzly bear." Grizz smiled as if he was proud of the moniker, but the expression was short-lived.

"Nah, it's because of his mean disposition," Pinky said, mockingly.

"What about you? I mean, Pinky? Where'd that come from?" she poked.

He raised both hands and on each pinky finger was a ring. Veronica looked at Grizz for his take. She wasn't disappointed.

"Just like I'm big, he's small, like a pinky!" The big man laughed loudly.

The small one barked at him. "You better check yourself, fat man. Just because I'm smaller than you, doesn't mean I ain't tough, you dummy."

Again, Grizz leaned in menacingly toward the smaller man. "And just because I'm large, doesn't mean I'm not smart, so don't test me. You'll lose."

Sensing both bears sufficiently poked, Veronica the peacemaker jumped in to ease the tension between the two. "Boys, please. Pinky, are you also from where Grizz calls home?"

Grizz jumped in to answer, "Are you kiddin' me? A guy this small would never make it on the streets I lived on!"

Pinky was not amused. "We invented the word 'tough' where I come from so you better hold yer tongue before I cut it out!" He produced a switchblade, popping the business end out. "I'm warning you…."

"Guys, guys. Let's simmer down and get back to our friendly card game."

Grizz acknowledged her request by shaking his head. Pinky, by putting his knife away.

"Now you guys are friends, you shouldn't be arguing over silly stuff. You are both smart, strong and might I say, handsome men." The diplomatic compliments seemed to lighten the mood as both men took relaxed positions and looked at their cards. Veronica wanted to continue gathering info but wanted to soothe the egos first so she lost the second game as well.

The third game, she won. "Would ya look at that!" she cried as she laid her cards down. "Is this where I say 'Gin?'" The two men turned from confident to sullen.

"Will ya stop giving her cards she can use, Grizz?" Pinky barked. "How do ya think I keep beating *you?*"

"How am I supposed to know what cards she needs?" Grizz said in reply. "I ain't no mind reader."

"You gotta watch what she picks up. She grabs a spade, spades are what she's looking for. A face card…"

Grizz broke in, "A face card is what she's lookin' for. I get it. Just shuffle and deal already."

Veronica picked up her cards and asked nonchalantly, "How did you guys get into this line of work?"

Both men looked at her through squinted eyes, neither answering.

"I find it fascinating, skirting the law and all. Don't you fear getting caught and going to jail?"

Grizz grunted at the question. "Jail? Been there, done that. You do your time, keep your mouth shut, and get out. Nuthin' to it."

Veronica noticed Pinky give Grizz a look she interpreted to say, 'You can shut up *now*.' Grizz missed it. "It's better than doing the suit and tie thing or workin' construction. Sure, we gotta take orders but I'd rather be sittin' here playin' cards than workin' on that construction site." He pointed a thumb toward the noise outside the building.

"GRIZZ!" shouted Pinky, giving him the 'shut up' look once more. "More card playin', less jabberin', capisce?"

Veronica held back a giggle. She knew where she'd get her information. She'd be patient and not so conspicuous with her intel gathering. She wasn't going anywhere now, but she was intent on leaving this place. And soon.

No longer intent on poking either bear, she purposely lost again. "Damn," she exclaimed. "Deal again."

The thugs, unaware of her ploy, happily complied.

After losing another two games, Veronica stood up. "Time for my chores. I'll start with the dishes." She walked to the sink and began washing. She whistled a happy tune to dull their suspicions but continued to take side glances to make sure they weren't watching her. *If only I could find something to write with...and on.*

Looking over at the table, she watched as Grizz wrote down another score. She couldn't very well just take the pen and paper from them, could she? *Or could she?* An idea appeared to make it plausible to do just that. She strode over to the table, grabbed the pen and pad, walked back over to the sink, and began to write.

"Hey!" yelled Grizz. "Whaddya think you're…"

"Will you relax, sweetie?" she replied, not looking up. "Next time you guys head out, you'll have a shopping list to bring with you. We need supplies." She wrote down a few cleaning items before announcing, "We're gonna need some more water. We're running low." She couldn't write the word 'Help!' Or anything resembling that. The message had to be understated so if the men did find the note, it wouldn't eliminate the trust she'd built with them. *Had to be subtle. Really subtle.*

Veronica knew it was a long shot but reasoned if someone from the construction site saw something out of place in the storage building, they might just investigate. If the goons found it, she'd claim she was just trying to spruce up the place and the paper got stuck somehow, confident they'd believe her. Not sure the old man would but this was a risk she felt was worth it.

She watched as both men looked over to where they kept the water, next to the refrigerator. Only a few bottles were left trapped in the plastic wrap that once housed twenty-four of them.

When Pinky chimed in, "Add some beer to the list. All this card playin' is making me thirsty, for Christ's sake." Veronica sighed in relief. They were giving her enough latitude to make certain decisions. And Pinky's request gave her an idea.

"Anything else?" she asked.

Grizz went over to the refrigerator, opened the door, and stuck his head in. This act also blocked Pinky's view. That's when Veronica lifted the list and turned to the last page of the notepad but did not write. Instead, she began to draw.

The ransom note was a plain piece of paper with the letters cut out of a magazine. Similar to ones seen on TV or in the movies. "Not very creative, are they?" Winnie complained.

Kennedy read the note aloud:

We have kidnapped Winnie Ahearne We demand million dollars from the Benton Estate and she ll be returned unharmed Do not go to the police or fa or you ll never see her again Stay tuned for more instructions

"Not very smart either," Winnie added.

"By now, I would assume they realize they have the wrong person," Kennedy interjected.

"We've got to go to the police." Axel was visibly nervous.

"No. They haven't done squat so far. What makes you think they'll find her? And if we go to the police, Well, read the damn note again," Winnie demanded, trying to take control.

Axel looked unsure, but Kennedy stepped forward. "Miss Winnie is right. Going to the authorities with this could put Veronica's life in danger."

Jules added, "Look, the police are out looking but we've solved one crime earlier this year. We can find Veronica as well and get her back safely."

Axel shot her a sharp look making Jules bow her head slightly. But this time Winnie didn't see deference. She saw fire in the eyes of the ex-marketing director. *Thatta girl.*

"So, as for the next step," Winnie jumped in. "I think…" She didn't finish her thought as this time, Axel interrupted *her.*

"Whoa, hold on. Winnie, you have too much on your plate. Now that we're here, we can take over to find Veronica."

Winnie knew coded speech when she heard it. "Too much on your plate," was a euphemism for, "You're too old," or "We're trying to protect you." She felt she didn't need protection.

"Whoa yourself, boyo," she barked. "Just because I'm elderly, doesn't mean I can't be of service. I have just as much right to be a part of this team as anybody. You aren't keeping me out of the loop."

Everyone looked at her with concern. "Miss Winnie," began Kennedy. "We appreciate you wanting to help, but we're concerned you might put yourself in danger."

Axel piled on, "Winnie, I lost my brother, I can't lose you, too."

Winnie looked over at Jules who remained silent. "You folks think that because you solved the last incident, you're the only ones qualified to solve this one as well?" She shuffled uncomfortably in her seat. "Let me tell you I was just as instrumental in capturing tha…"

Axel slapped his hands on her desk. "Winnie, it's settled. You stay here safe and sound where Hector can protect you and we'll do what's necessary to bring our girl back."

Winnie stared at Axel, saying through clenched teeth, "Blessed are those who get prosecuted like the prophets before them."

"No one is prosec…*persecuting* you. We just want you to be safe," Axel said, correcting the phrase.

Winnie was about to protest further until Axel lifted a hand from the desk. "Enough. We don't need two missing persons here. It is settled."

Winnie took a deep breath, realizing this path was blocked. She needed another.

"All right," she said, her tone turned submissive. "If you think that's best." She gave back the control she had usurped earlier. *For now.*

"We do!" the two men chimed in. Jules was still silent but gave Winnie a raised eyebrow. She knows me too well, Winnie thought.

"OK, good luck. But if you'll indulge a helpless old woman one thought, I think you'll find the advice sound." Winnie had recalled Kepner's warning: "*Interfering with an ongoing investigation is a crime.*"

Axel's shoulders drooped. He shot a glance at the other two before turning back to Winnie. "Go ahead," he sighed. "What's on your mind?"

"Mr. Kennedy, if I were you, I'd put the ransom note back where you found it," she began. "Just like Veronica's phone and keys, when it comes time to bring in the authorities, we want to claim culpable deniability, don't we?"

The three looked at her with puzzled expressions, so she continued her train of thought.

"Not sharing important details with an ongoing investigation could be viewed as obstruction, could it not? And what kind of sentence would something like that carry?"

Kennedy grinned at the old woman's guile. "Good call, Miss Winnie. I'll put it back as soon as we get back to Veronica's. When it's time, I'll alert the authorities I found something."

"Good. Don't fret, I'll be right here if you need me for anything else."

As the three left her office, Winnie sat at her desk happy with her ruse. An old saying from her father came to mind. She changed it to the feminine to suit her needs. *She who keeps her tongue keeps her friends.*

She believed this saying also included family members and even though she didn't want to oversell it, she added just enough resignation to her voice to satisfy them. And then say no more. Would they never learn? You couldn't persecute Winnie Ahearne. When she put her mind to something, it would take more than her friends and relatives to stop her. Now she had to figure out what *her* next step would be. A thought came to mind as she opened the laptop on her desk and typed Benton Falls Docket. Up popped the business licenses, governmental meetings, and so forth of everyday life in a small town. She searched for real estate: Recent rentals, purchases, or leases. Anything that would suggest newly acquired property. Especially property that was a perfect prison to hold a pregnant woman. Secluded, quiet, and most of all, inconspicuous.

Winnie, despite the protests of her family, wasn't about to leave the important work to them. And this was the perfect first step. If keeping one's tongue kept one's friends, it could also help to keep one pregnant lady alive.

Assistant Chief Nick Holmes scowled. As a veteran of over twenty-five years on the Benton Falls police force, he'd seen his share of crimes. He'd also been relentless about solving them. He was well aware of how he got the nickname, "Bulldog." Secretly he liked the tough-sounding moniker. However, he was not going to let on he liked it. No one ever called him this to his face and he reveled in his prowess to intimidate criminals and policemen alike. Having a badass reputation was a good tool for doing things his way when it came to fighting crime in this city.

He shook his head as he looked over the case file before him. He loved solving robberies. Enjoyed busting up drug rings. Apprehending criminals. He understood crimes and those who committed them. They kept him employed. But there was one case he abhorred. One crime he hated more than anything. Kidnapping.

It made his blood boil. Taking someone against their will was immoral business. Bulldog felt it was the worst crime this side of murder. It was cowardly.

The chief had tasked him with finding Veronica Bucholtz, who had gone missing recently. He remembered she was related somehow to Winnie Ahearne. *That crazy old woman.*

He recalled the events from earlier this year when the Ahearne woman with the help of her grandson and his girl-friend stopped a serial killer at the nursing home. She may be crazy but everyone underestimated her. The last casualty was her grandson, who was turning his shady life around when it happened and now someone had taken his girlfriend.

He scanned the files and saw the victim had left everything in her home intact. No suitcases were missing, the car sat in the driveway, and not a single cell call after a last text to her employer. Not even a bank transaction was recorded. All signs pointing to a kidnapping. One note caught his eye. She was also pregnant. The heat began to rise on his face. The rats had abducted not only the woman but the baby she carried. What pieces of shit would do that? *Cowards, that's who.*

There were pieces of the puzzle that didn't make sense. The case had all the markings of a kidnapping with two glaring exceptions: One, what was the kidnapper's motive? Money? She had a job as a nurse and some other income sources, but nothing worth a jail term. Love triangle? Didn't seem likely with a pregnant woman. Vendetta? This motive seemed preposterous. And two, no ransom note. What kind of kidnappers didn't ask for something for the safe return of their prey?

His next thought was even more infuriating. What if the coward(s) only wanted what the young woman could give? Was there another serial killer on the loose in Benton Falls? A psycho like the whack job who killed all those innocent old people at the FALM earlier this year? Even though Bulldog wanted to check off all the boxes, this was one box he didn't even want to consider. It was too heinous.

Bulldog buried his nose back into the file and began to formulate a plan of attack.

His first step was to search the Ahearne house once again where the woman was last located. Then speak with the relatives and finally the neighbors to find out if there were any witnesses to suspicious activity; strangers on the sidewalk, a car looking out of place. Any clue he could sink his teeth into.

He closed the file and shook his head, determined to find the woman alive and save her from the dirtbags who did this.

He also knew whoever perpetrated this crime would not survive his wrath.

After all, he was the Bulldog, and not only did he abhor kidnappings. He absolutely abhorred kidnappers. He sneered as he verbally reiterated this last point, "The cowards."

Axel and Jules drove to Veronica's house. Kennedy argued that if they had a base of operations, it would be easier to plan. Plus, there was plenty of room for all.

"You're being insensitive," Jules told Axel.

"What are you talking about?" asked a perplexed Axel.

"Winnie is trying to help find Veronica and you are shutting her out."

Axel got defensive. "No, I'm not, I'm protecting her."

"Protecting her? She's tougher than anyone I know. Did you forget how she helped us stop the killings at the FALM? She was fearless!"

Axel shook his head. "And fearlessness almost got her killed. No, she has to stay out of this…"

Jules stopped him with a raised hand. "She's smart, and savvy and has great ideas. You should at least hear her out. How can advice be dangerous?"

Axel rubbed his hand through his hair and let out a big sigh. "Jules, the woman is old and frail. In order to keep her safe, I have to keep her at arm's length. The kidnappers left a note admitting she was the target, so the only way I know how to protect Winnie is to keep her at the FALM with Hector and out of our plans. That's final."

"Well, now you're just being an ass. And not only to her but to me as well. Do you know you barked at or interrupted me several times today?"

"I did? I thought I was just making my points clear." Axel wasn't used to being spoken to this way. Since taking on Leif's seminars, he'd grown accustomed to being in charge and Jules had taken a back seat. It seemed as though Jules no longer liked the view from there.

"Well, you did. I don't know what's gotten into you lately, but I don't like it."

"C'mon," he said, softening his tone. "You know how much she means to me. To all of us. Even you believe she needs protection." As an afterthought, said "And you do, too."

"That's ridiculous. The kidnappers probably don't even know I exist. *Here's* what I believe. In the last few months, you've been the alpha male. Delivering the seminars and running Leif's business. In charge of the Benton estate. Now you're trying to run a rescue operation. You can't do all this by yourself."

"Alpha male?" Axel questioned.

"Yes. Like you're the one in control." Jules bit her upper lip. "You have to stop treating us women as though we are porcelain dolls. We can hold our own and you know it."

He went to pat her hand but stopped short so as not to seem condescending. "Yes, you're tough as nails." He paused before asking, "I'm not really an ass, am I?"

"No, but sometimes you act like it. We really should at least listen to her. She needs to feel she's contributing. As do I."

Axel nodded. It was the best he could do at this point. He had no intention of letting the women in his life get involved in this nasty business. This was a job for him and Kennedy.

Nodding would give her the assurances she needed to move on and him the culpable deniability he sought. He'd lost his brother and was not going to lose either of the women he loved.

Porcelain, he thought, isn't the only thing that breaks.

"Axel, where are we with the investigation?" Winnie asked, the frustration in her voice evident. "Any leads?" She heard Axel clear his throat before answering. "Not yet, but Kennedy and I are working feverishly on this. We're looking at the real estate dockets for leads, you know, like a manufacturing plant out of town or a secluded house in the country."

Still a step behind, thought Winnie. These leads had already failed to produce any clues.

"Won't find anything, I already looked." *Persecute me, will ya?*

Axel was curt. "Winnie, I know you want to help, but Kennedy and I are on top of this. We're doing everything we can to find her. You let us do the worrying and looking. I need you to stay safe."

Winnie began to protest. "But I…"

"No buts. We're on it. We've had this discussion. Look, I have to get back to work. Talk to you later."

The line buzzed in her ear as anger arose in her face. "That's it!" she yelled. "If he doesn't want my help, so be it. But I'm not some old nag to be put out to pasture."

She cradled the phone back in place and took a deep, calming breath. "God helps those who help others," she whispered, unaware of her miscue. "And I need to help Veronica."

Hector knocked on Winnie's door. "Got a minute to talk, boss?" Winnie winced, giving him a stern look. "I don't know how many times I have to tell you. Please don't call me that, Hector. It makes me feel uncomfortable. After what we've been through, first names should come easily."

Hector bowed his head and uttered, "Sorry, Miss Winnie." Lifting it back up, he asked, "Any news on Veronica?"

Winnie shook her head. "So far nothing on Veronica's whereabouts," she began. "So, I need your help. Axel, Jules, and Kennedy have shut me out of trying to find her."

"And you want me to help you disobey them?"

"No, not disobey, assist. If you think I'm gonna sit on my hands and not even try, you are sadly mistaken. We've got to find Vee and her unborn baby now! And you..." she said, pointing a finger at him, "must keep this between us. I don't need any more lectures from my grandson."

Hector bowed to Winnie, which she saw as a good sign. "I am at your service, Boss lady, command me."

"There you go again," she said, shaking her head. She was taken by this young man. It was hard not to be. He was trustworthy, loyal, and honest. She hated to use him as a shield against her grandson, but didn't the end justify the means?

"First things first, I've checked the real estate portion of the docket and came up empty. I need to get a map of all the buildings on the outskirts of town. You know, the ones that are either empty or have little traffic. The perfect place to hold a kidnap victim."

"An abstract company," said Hector. "I have a friend who works for one. I could give him a call."

"A what?" she asked.

"Abstract company. They search for titles, and proof of ownership. And have better connections than you or I. That might give us something to work with."

"Perfect! Get on that right away and report back." Winnie waved Hector off and he headed for the door, but she stopped him. "Wait, you wanted a word?"

Hector bit his lip as he walked over to her desk. "I uh, wanted to know if you got any packages lately?"

"As a matter of fact, your timing is perfect! I have something for you." Smiling, she produced a small white box and handed it to him.

"My Tag-It!" he said, grinning broadly. He took it out and attached it to the key chain he produced from his pocket. "I'll go back to my office and sync it up right now!"

"Don't forget to check with your friend at the… What did you call it? Abacus?"

"*Abstract* company." Hector slid through the door but peeked his head back in. "Thanks, boss!" he said, jiggling his keys at her with the Tag-It! attached.

Winnie let out a little laugh. Watching Hector's excitement was heartwarming. Making her employees and residents happy was a positive perk of her job. Maybe being the boss wasn't a bad thing after all.

Will checked in on Benton as part of his rounds. He came into the room with a large plastic bag but upon seeing the old man had soiled himself again, placed the bag on the chair in the corner and began the cleanup. Reaching into the plastic bag, he made it easier for the next time by putting an adult diaper on the man. Now clean up only included the diaper and not the sheets.

"You do like to make it interesting, don't you?"

Benton looked mournful and embarrassed.

"Don't worry. I'm here to care for you. Not your fault," Will said as he finished. "Say, I've been doing some research…" Will paused to see if the old man reacted. He wasn't disappointed. Benton leaned in, listening.

"I have two presents for you." Will went back to the plastic bag and retrieved a box. He opened it and showed the old man his prize. It was a blue glove with wires attached to a small white box. From the box, two wires protruded with electrode tabs at each end.

Will slipped the blue glove on the old man's right hand before attaching the electrodes to his damaged left hand. When he turned the switch on, Benton flinched.

"It's called Electronic Stimulation Therapy. You move your right hand and the connection tells your brain to move your left hand. Been in clinical trials so it's mainly used for arthritis patients. The jury is still out but hey, it's promising." Will watched as the old man made a fist, then relaxed. Then repeated. The fingers on his left hand moved slightly inward.

"Well, it's a start. What do you think?" Will said. The old man gave a half smile.

"Look, I ran it by the physical therapist and she said it wasn't part of your regimen so you and I can work on it during my visits. I just thought we'd see if it works to restore that left hand of yours."

Benton stopped his hand motion and raised his good hand. Will saw he had two fingers lifted.

"Two? Not sure I understand?"

Benton dropped the middle finger back into his fist, leaving his index digit standing.

"One. OK." Will was still confused until Benton lifted both hands as if he had handcuffs attached.

"Oh, sorry," Will exclaimed as he now understood. "The glove was number one. Are you ready for the second?"

Benton nodded and reached out his good hand and patted the young man on the arm. Will pulled a note from his pocket and handed it to Benton.

"It's from my mom," Will said. "You wanna tell me what you and my mom have cooking?" Will was anxious to find out what was transpiring between the two but wouldn't think of betraying their trust in him.

Benton shook his head while reading. When finished, he folded it back to its original shape and handed the note back for disposal. Will stuffed the note in his pocket.

Benton's attempt at a smile was weak, but Will recognized it. The old man had also lifted his left hand clasped into his right and nodded slowly. It reminded Will of a yoga instructor bowing in deference.

*Namaste- I bow to you.*

This gesture warmed Will's heart. "You keep practicing with the gloves and remember our secret."

Bowing back to the old man, his own hands clasped together, Will said, "Mr. Benton, I promised to take care of you. And I never break a promise."

Getting up to leave, he turned back towards Benton and bowed once more. "Never," he repeated, before exiting the room.

Kennedy sat at the kitchen table of Veronica's home. A just poured cup of coffee steamed to his right, and a pile of papers sat to his left. These were no ordinary papers. He had tasked himself to scour every one looking for the name of each person listed and digging into the story of why they were written on these pages.

Harley Benton had kept a secret ledger of those who either owed him money, or favors. When the police needed evidence to root out corruption in Benton Falls, including their own department, Kennedy turned the ledger over to the one man he felt was honest enough to handle the information correctly. Detective Gary Kepner. Kepner followed up on the leads the ledger provided and not only exposed the corruption in the town but landed the job of the Chief of Police for his efforts.

It was true Kennedy had turned over the ledger to Detective Kepner. That news had made the local paper and was common knowledge. But not all the contents were included. Only the pages exposing corruption. The pages on his left were carefully extracted from the ledger due to their content. Those people who had done nothing but ask for a helping hand from the old codger. Or were being extorted by the evil man Kennedy once called his employer. Kepner didn't need those names. But Kennedy did and he would go through each case as if it was the most important one and work to right the wrongs. Axel had forgiven him and now, with the work he was undertaking, he hoped God would see fit as well. Kennedy took pleasure in what the incapacitated Benton would think of his task. Not likely would the old man take it lightly. He could rot in the FALM's Passing Lane, as far as the ex-butler was concerned.

He justified his actions by telling himself he was providing a service to his community by delivering the necessary evidence that restored an honest (well, mostly) town leadership. Secondly, effectively ending Harley Benton's grip on the disadvantaged and unfortunate people from his beloved town. This included his own freedom from the clutches of the diabolical Benton. He had also been a victim, paying off an old debt by working as the old man's butler. This was not a debt of money, but one of silence.

Benton had first-hand knowledge of Kennedy's crime and used coercion and extortion to press the young Kennedy into service all these years. He knew too well the helpless feeling of extortion and vowed to free others from its detestable grip. There was only one path to forgiving himself for allowing the manipulation.

Kennedy understood full well the dealings of the old man and how he used information to gain profit, leverage, and control. The ex-butler had wondered how the old man had collected his ill-gotten gains and found out about the post office box that collected the checks from Benton's lawyer, who had stayed on to help Axel and Kennedy with the running of Benton's estate after his stroke. Previously, the lawyer would stop by from time to time to discuss business with the old man. Part of that business was handing over the contents of said mailbox.

Kennedy scanned each page, making notes in a separate notebook. He put a finger next to one victim's name, Mr. Greg

Hoell, who seemed to be a hard-working family man. Mr. Hoell had asked Benton for a bridge loan to help him pay his bills while he awaited a check from his insurance company for an auto injury not his fault. The accident left Greg disabled and unable to work for a period of time, crippling not only the man but his ability to provide for his growing family. Having a low credit score didn't fare well with the local banks so he approached Harley Benton. Little did Hoell know, Benton added a usurious interest rate that not only weakened the bridge but caused it to tumble into the abyss of untenable debt. Even turning over the whole insurance check made little dent in the rising principal owed.

This was Harley Benton's way of controlling poorer folk. Trap them in debt, then add them to his minion's list. Those who didn't cooperate faced financial ruin. Kennedy found many who would bend to Benton's rule. He found no one who fought back. Until he took on the task.

Writing on a plain piece of paper, Kennedy outlined his idea of a repayment plan.

*Dear Mr. Hoell,*

*I know these past few years have been difficult for you since your accident. I understand you've recovered sufficiently and have not only returned to your previous place of employment but have also taken on additional work. Your work ethic and commitment to your family is admirable. I have reviewed your case and decided to retire your debt to Harley Benton in full.*

*Please cease making any more payments to the PO Box you were provided, as it is no longer necessary.*

*Any amounts in transit will be returned. You are free from all debts to Benton and his business interests.*

*I only ask a few things of you. One, that you hold this conversation in the strictest of confidence and destroy this letter promptly, as I've destroyed any trace of your debt from my end.*

*Secondly, The next time you need to borrow money, seek out reputable financial institutions.*

*Lastly, try to pass on a good deed to another as I have done so for you, for one good deed truly deserves another.*

*Good luck in the future.*
*Estate of Harley Benton*

The language of destroying the letter left him vaguely satisfied. It made no difference whether or not they eliminated the evidence, most would probably hold on to the letter as proof, but he reveled in the intrigue. Adding his request for a good deed was a nice touch; proud he could pass on a little bit of happiness to his fellow town folk.

It was true Kennedy would destroy the page from the ledger with Mr. Hoell's name on it. But he had a secret plan he was unwilling to share with anyone. Yet.

Returning to his task, Kennedy sealed the letter and placed a stamp on it. It was the last letter from the page. Picking up his pen, he crossed the man's name from the page and set it aside for disposal. Benton could no longer hold the debt over the man's head. Not that it would matter as he rotted away in the Passing Lane of the FALM. Kennedy smiled at the thought that Karma had delivered the perfect sentence to the old criminal.

He looked at the pile to his left as he sipped his cooling coffee, taking a deep breath before continuing the work ahead. The effort was rewarding yet tiresome. He had seen firsthand the treachery and greed of Benton and the effect this wicked man had on the community. Part of Kennedy's self-imposed penance for staying in the orbit of this monster was to right the wrongs of the old man. And the lists helped soothe his own guilt and complicity.

Mr. Kennedy rose and went to the coffee pot to refill his cup before he returned to the table where he picked up the next piece of Harley Benton's secret ledger. He scanned the list briefly until he came to a name that stopped him cold. Leif Ahearne.

The usually unflappable Kennedy was shocked to discover Axel's brother had borrowed money from Benton. *How did this escape my attention?* After cleverly watching over the old employer, he felt he knew most of the workings of the old man's business. Missing this piece of information felt like he had betrayed Axel. Kennedy surmised this as the reason the young man had started writing. To get the money for repayment. His success was one good thing to come from the old man's corruption.

Axel would have to learn about this activity eventually and Kennedy had every intention of discussing this procedure with him when the time was right. If he hadn't found the ransom note, this fact could have been a solid argument as to why Veronica was abducted.

For the time being, he decided he would exclude his brother's name from the discussion with Axel, not wanting to hurt his friend any more than he already had. It was a moot point anyway. Dead men couldn't repay anything. And a certain stroke patient no longer had use of these debts. Crossing out Leif's name was only a formality. Once he finished writing letters to the rest of the names on the list, he would destroy any evidence of its existence.

Finding the next name on the list, Kennedy shook his head at the debtor and debt owed. It would seem even judges were not immune from borrowing money. *Unbelievable.*

He wrote a similar note to the judge, making sure it didn't sound accusatory. One didn't know the full extent of the arrangement between the two, and Kennedy hoped it hadn't resulted in any unfair court rulings. As he addressed the envelope, he made a mental note to cross-reference any incoming mail with a return address he suspected was on the list and mark it return to sender. All correspondence and the contents of such would then be returned to its rightful owner. Mr. Kennedy's next thought produced a satisfying grin. *Ah, to be a fly on the wall when Benton finds out what I've done.*

Moving on to the next name on the list, and then addressing the envelope, he continued his task. Licking his thumb, he ran it across a blank sheet of paper to pick it up and place it in front of him. He looked up, squinting as he thought, then began to write.

At the same time Kennedy was writing his letters, the lawyer of Benton's estate, Harold Grange, sat at his own desk thinking about the weekend. He had plans to take a certain young lady kayaking below the falls on Saturday. They'd been dating almost a year but it had been chaotic. And exciting. Several years her senior, he questioned what she saw in him. She was beautiful, fit, and always on the go. He could hardly keep up with her. Although grateful, a nagging feeling persisted. He pushed back the unpleasant thought she might be with him just for the money. The arrangement was that he'd pay for her apartment and a small stipend and she would see him exclusively. He resisted the urge to get a private detective to have her followed. Not ready to go there just yet. But lately, after days filled with working out, hiking, or other physical activities, she had become less enthusiastic in the bedroom.

The phone rang, pushing those thoughts to the side. "Mr... Grange?" said a voice Harold did not recognize. It sounded gravelly. Old.

"Yes, this is he. And who is this?"

"That is of no consequence," stated the voice.

Harold sighed. He hated these calls from people looking for pro bono work or worse, thinking they had a million-dollar case not worth ten cents believing they were so important that their identity had to be hidden. "Look, I'm a very busy man…"

The voice interrupted, "Then I'll take it you do not wish to represent the Harley Benton estate any further?" This question grabbed Harold's attention. Harold Grange had been Harley's attorney for the last fifteen years. Even though the old man was incapacitated, the hefty retainer was still being honored by the new overseer, Axel Ahearne.

"Now wait a second, I deal with Mr. Ahearne on matters concerning Mr. Benton. Who is this again?" Harold grimaced at the sound of the old man's voice. As if the person on the line was ancient.

"Suffice it to say with the information I have, Mr. Ahearne will have to relinquish his authority back to Mr. Benton in good haste. You see, it has come to my attention that the will you have on file was never signed by Mr. Benton."

"That's not true. And if you hold on one moment, I'll pull the document."

"Please," said the voice. "By all means."

Harold walked to a file cabinet and opened it. He found the document and took it back to his desk. "Mister, I have it right here in my hands. Signed and sealed by Mr. Harley Benton."

"Ah, but is it? Have you done your due diligence?" asked the voice.

"I don't know what game you're playing but I don't have to…"

"This is no game, I assure you. Did you have the alleged signature looked at by a handwriting expert?"

"No. Why would I do that? I've worked in concert with Mr. Benton for years. Well, until he took ill. I know what his signature looks like."

Harold heard a chuckle. "Do you, Mister Grange? Do you? My suggestion is you find a reputable handwriting expert to either confirm your claim… or my suspicion."

"And if I don't?" Harold was good at playing these types of games. Crank calls were a part of the job description.

"Then, I'll take matters into my own hands and prove this signature is not Mr. Benton's. Are you willing to take the chance that it is a forgery? Because if I prove it is, this will not end well for you. Your retainer will cease and close the books on your relationship with the Benton estate. Who knows what else could happen? Malpractice? Even disbarment?"

Harold froze. Usually, he could easily dispense with the cranks, but the old man on the other end of the phone had planted a seed. This old man was certainly not familiar with the law. Grange could easily prove he was not a party to any fraud if it came to that. However, if the signature *was* false and he did not uncover it, his gravy train would come to an end. He didn't fear disbarment. But he did fear derailment.

"You've convinced me to investigate, sir. For Mr. Benton's sake. I take pride in defending my clients and if your assertions are correct, I'll help remedy the situation. You have my word."

"Good. I thought you'd see things my way. I'll be in touch." The dial tone replaced the voice. Harold, shaken at the thought of losing his best client, began searching for a reputable handwriting expert. All thoughts of his lady friend and his suspicions of her potential infidelity paled in comparison to the thoughts of losing this small fortune. Crank call or not, nothing was more important than maintaining the revenue stream generated by one Harley Benton, incapacitated or not.

Searching on his browser for the term 'Handwriting expert,' he found a few reputable contacts. He picked up the phone and dialed the first number.

"Hello," he said once answered. "My name is Harold Grange. I have information I'd like you to look at regarding Mr. Harley Benton."

# Chapter Eight

Kennedy was worried. As were all the people close to Veronica. But he had a job to do and because it was his duty, he went back to Benton Manor to oversee the tourists who would be traipsing through the house and grounds. It was a relief to think of something other than kidnapping or any of the possible outcomes that went with it.

At first glance, Kennedy and Axel believed opening Benton Manor to the public would be of interest only to the local population, perhaps even within the state. What they found was the estate had become an attraction outside the realm of the curious townsfolk. Harley Benton's home attracted tourists from every state and even from other countries. Both men marveled at the increased interest, even though its last occupant, albeit handicapped, was still alive. Neither could have predicted the appetite for exploring the grounds and home of the town's benefactor or the need to hire more docents to share stories from the Benton family through the ages. This development did not hinder Kennedy's desire to continue giving tours. In fact, because of his previous employment with the historic manor's owner, he was highly sought after to tell authentic firsthand stories. He excelled in the role as a former butler and now, favorite docent.

Today, he met the next group at the appointed time, thankful for the distraction from Veronica's plight.

"Welcome to Benton Manor," he announced. "It is my pleasure to have you here and hope by the time you're ready to leave, the pleasure will be all yours." He bowed and with a sweep of his right arm, invited the tourists into the grand home.

"I am your host today and will provide the background for this estate and its past occupants. But first, we're waiting on a few late guests. In the meantime, may I invite you to wait in the foyer?"

Benton Manor never looked so good. Even though he was butler to Harley Benton and had to make sure the Manor was tidy, he now had a staff of people who would do the heavy cleaning. He made sure they were thorough, yet treated all who worked there fairly, remembering how he, himself, was treated by the evil lord for nearly twenty-five years. *No one should have to go through that type of abuse.*

He truly enjoyed playing the part, dressed in his butler attire, telling stories, answering questions, and showing off this grand home for all to enjoy. He left out the darker side of the manor, forsaking Harley Benton's sordid history, for a cleaner, more palatable, yet still interesting one. The act was such a hit, that he required the other docents to dress similarly as part of the household staff. He helped each docent polish stories and offered intimate knowledge of the place to be shared with guests.

"And here we have the library, where Benton men conducted business since the home was built. Wouldn't we just love to have been privy to some of those conversations, yes?"

Kennedy thought of his spying place, where he would eavesdrop on his former boss, unseen or heard, making sure to leave that space out of the tale.

"Where is the latest Benton now?" asked one woman, apparently from out of town. She gazed out the library window towards the family cemetery in the back corner of the property.

Most of the townsfolk in Benton Falls knew he wasn't resting there. Yet. They knew exactly where he lay.

"I'm afraid, Mr. Harley Benton has been incapacitated by a stroke and is a current resident in the Benton Falls adult facility in town. But he did leave a most gracious gift."

Kennedy wondered what Benton would think of such a gift: Allowing 'commoners' to ramble through his house and grounds at will. The ex-butler surmised the old man wouldn't care for it at all. The elderly Benton was not the gifting type. But it was Kennedy's forgery on Benton's will that delivered the gift to all who would want to see how the one percent lived.

Now that Benton no longer had power over him and recognizing the slim chance Kennedy could be exposed as the forger continued to get slimmer, he sighed in relief before continuing.

"You are enjoying the gift now. I hope you come to appreciate the sacrifice the last Benton made so folks such as yourself could enjoy this grand home and its wondrous gardens and lawn." Axel had scoffed at the notion Kennedy should offer the credit to Harley Benton. Kennedy explained it better to be welcoming to guests rather than prideful to an empty home.

The doorbell rang so Kennedy bowed as he excused himself to add the latecomers onto the tour. He opened the door with a flourish and began, "Welcome to Benton Manor." Before he had a chance to continue, the large man put a hand against the door so Kennedy couldn't shut it.

"Are you Kennedy?" he asked brusquely.

"Why yes, I am. But I'm afraid I'm indisposed at the moment. I'm giving a tour. Are you here to join us?"

A badge was held up in Kennedy's face. "Assistant Police Chief Nick Holmes. And I'm afraid I don't give a shit about your tour. I need you to come down to the station to answer some questions."

"Concerning what, may I inquire?" Kennedy said, steadfast in keeping his composure. The only tell he was nervous came from the sweat forming on his upper lip.

"Not until we get to the station," barked the officer. "So, we can do it peacefully. Or we can do it the hard way. Your choice. Either way, you're coming with me."

Kennedy now recognized the detective turned assistant police chief. He also dreaded that the conversation would revolve around a certain signature on a certain will, his earlier idea of the chance of the forgery coming to light just increased tenfold. But ever the professional, Kennedy kept his head held high. He pulled a handkerchief from his pocket and wiped his lips.

"Very good sir. We'll do it the easy way," Kennedy said with a nod. "But first, let me get someone to take care of these tourists if you please." He took a cell from his pocket and called one of the staff members to come and relieve him. Then he stepped out the front door and accompanied the large officer to his car as the late group of tourists hurried past him. He smiled and pointed the way through the open door. Turning back towards the police car, the smile disappeared as he slid into the back seat.

As the car pulled away, Kennedy, now firmly in the grasp of the Bulldog, wondered if the bite was strong enough to send him to prison.

———

Hector stood by Winnie's desk and looked over her shoulder at her cell phone screen. "Show me how this Tag-It! thingy works, Will you? My mind is going and you'll never know when I'll start losing things," she said convincingly. She didn't share with Hector her true reason for keeping one of these gadgets.

"Oh, Miss Winnie, you're sharper than most young people I know. Heck, you'll probably outlive us all, too!"

"Please don't wish *that* on me," she replied. "Now. How do we set this doodad up?"

Taking her cell phone, Hector downloaded the Tag-It! App. He registered it in her name and began the process of linking the small device to her phone. "Here is the app," he said, pointing to her screen. "Touch it."

The app opened to show the word 'List.' "See where it says, 'Winnie's Tag-It!?' Tap that and voila! A screen pops up. That green dot is this," he explained, holding the small device in the air.

"I'm going to walk down the hall. You should see the green dot moving. That's me. Be back in a minute," he said as he left her office. Sure enough, a green dot moved along and away from her office. The screen was filled with the location of the FALM and surrounding streets. Winnie marveled at how technology had changed since her childhood, noticing the green dot changing direction as Hector returned to her office.

"Didja see it?" he asked, like an excited little boy pointing out his first airplane sighting.

"Amazing," Winnie crowed. "But tell me. How do I find it?"

Pointing to her screen, he replied, "Easy. See the street level near the green dot? That's where we are. Now as you get closer, tap this "Find Me" tab." He did so and the screen turned purple. He moved the device farther from the phone. A number appeared showing the distance in feet. The number grew larger as he moved away, and smaller as he moved closer.

"The screen is too small. I can't see the larger map," Winnie complained.

"Easy fix," said Hector. He pinched his thumb and index finger together, touched the screen, and opened them. The screen showed more surface of the surrounding area. "You try."

After Winnie had mastered the pinch, she said, "I think I've got the gist. Thanks for setting it up for me."

Hector asked one more question before leaving. "What object are you going to use it for, keys, luggage?"

Winnie smirked, waving for him to get back to work. "I'll think of something, my dear. Nothing too valuable. Any word from your friend at the abstract company?"

Hector went over to Winnie's laptop and pulled up her email. "Here is what he sent me. I had him CC you."

Each file sent had an address. Opening a PDF showed the construction blueprint of the project. The address was at the top next to the project ownership. Scrolling through each one, she exclaimed, "Hector, these are all new projects. And close to the city limits. Aren't there any old structures like a man-ufacturing plant that has recently changed hands? Someplace out of the way?"

Hector shrugged his shoulders. "Let me ask him. There is a lot of new building going on, just not what you were looking for?"

"Nope. Not even close." Winnie now had to shift gears. Think, she thought. *Where could one hide a pregnant woman?* The captors had to be somewhere with little traffic, somewhere out of the way where they wouldn't arouse suspicion. But where? She felt as blind as the mice in the nursery rhyme.

"Any other ideas?" she asked Hector.

"No, ma'am. I'm sorry. Do you need anything else?"

Winnie thought a moment before responding. "Not now. I'll call you if I need you."

Hector walked to the door and opened it.

"Oh, Hector?" Winnie said. "Thank you."

Hector nodded his head in gratitude and closed the door behind him.

Now alone, Winnie picked up the Tag-It! turning it over in her fingers.

"Blessed are the pure in heart, for they shall see God," she whispered. Winnie didn't want to see God. Not just yet. What she wanted was to see Veronica again. Alive.

Some dangerous people had abducted Veronica and, according to the ransom note, had intentions to nab her as well. The kidnappers had caught her off guard when they took Vee, but if they did reach her, Winnie didn't want to leave her friends in the dark. "This blind mouse plans on leaving breadcrumbs," she whispered, slipping the Tag-It! into her pocket.

Before his shift ended, Will slipped into Benton's room to say goodnight. The young man pulled a chair up by the bedside and began to talk to the old one. He spoke of his childhood, where he was raised, some high school memories, and his dreams for the future. Benton seemed to enjoy this one-sided conversation and Will found pleasure in these visits as well. He hated that Harley Benton, the town's benefactor, would waste away in this facility with no human interaction. It wasn't right. Even though the visit usually lasted around thirty minutes or so each evening, he committed himself to not only spend time with the old man but to engage him with conversation and the gloves. Both stimulating.

Will talked nonstop as his elderly patient listened intently, feeling it necessary to keep his side of the conversation going without any awkward pauses. He knew Benton could write, but it was sometimes too cumbersome to have a conversation this way. A one-word question would prompt Will to try and discern what Benton meant. When he was right, the conversation went smoothly. When wrong, frustration would bubble up, which tired the old man. Will wished Benton could engage in a verbal conversation. *If ifs were skiffs, we'd all be sailing,* he heard his mother say, her voice clear in his head. The disappointment was something he was used to.

Growing up in a single-parent home wasn't the best of situations, but the two had made it work. Benton had become somewhat of a grandfather figure to him and he relished the time spent together. Will knew the man used to be rich. Now he was just waiting to die. A fact Will found saddening. And that was precisely why he spent more with the old man than anyone else in the building. He was committed to making Harley Benton's last days positive. Anything else but lonely.

Will got up to leave and patted a sleepy Benton on the arm. "I'll check on you in the morning," he said, optimistically.

He reached for the door and turned to the old man before opening it. "G'night," he whispered.

Will stopped in his tracks as he heard a noise from his bedridden patient's direction. *Was it his imagination?* Benton could make the occasional guttural sounds but was not able to utter normal words. Or could he? Will decided to test the old man.

"I said, *good night*." This time the response was more than a whisper. It was clear, crisp, and other than a missing consonant at the end, clearly the correct answer.

"Nigh," Benton repeated. Then after realizing what he'd done, both eyes opened wide. The right one wider than the left, but still better than normal. Will's smile was broad enough for both of them. This was no time to leave. It was a time for miracles. He shut the door behind him and walked back to Benton's bedside.

"Will wonders never cease. Welcome back," he said.

Busted, the old man decided to take his time to answer loud and clear. "Goo too be bah."

Kennedy sat in the sparse concrete interrogation room. One table, two chairs, and a mirror on one of the walls. On the table sat a yellow legal pad and pen. He chuckled. It was like being in an episode of every TV crime drama. Usually, the detectives of such shows parade a variety of suspects into a similar room and grill them all in an attempt to ferret out answers and a confession. And to confuse the viewer as to who was the real criminal. Only this time, Kennedy was the perp. And by his own admission, guilty. A secret he hoped he could keep.

Nick Holmes, AKA the Bulldog, came into the interrogation room and sat down across from Kennedy. With a pen of his own, pushed the pen within Kennedy's grasp, before placing his back in his shirt pocket. Kennedy knew why the assistant chief had done that. *Fingerprints.*

Kennedy was aware Harley Benton's will would indeed have his fingerprints all over the document. He also knew that anyone else who handled it would have theirs as well; the lawyer, Axel, and even Harley himself. He picked up the pen with his left hand and clicked it, ready to write whatever the Bulldog wanted. Well, this side of a confession.

"I'd like you to write your name here," Bulldog requested, pointing a finger at the top left of the pad without actually touching it. Kennedy complied.

"Now I want you to write the name of your last employer," he ordered.

Kennedy began writing "The Benton Museum Foundation," when Bulldog barked at him, "No, no. The one before that! And in cursive."

Kennedy wrote, *Axel Ahe…* before he was stopped again.

"*Before that!*" Bulldog said, the exasperation in his voice showing. Kennedy knew exactly what the officer wanted, but decided the best defense was a good offense. And by the look on the Bulldog's face, he was offended.

"Are you referring to Mr. Benton, sir?" he asked.

Bulldog bit his lower lip in frustration. "Yes, exactly who I meant."

Kennedy hid a grin. He understood that keeping one's head when others do not, gave one the upper hand. "Like this?" he inquired, looking innocently at the large man.

Bulldog took the pen from his pocket using it to spin the pad around, careful not to touch it, and looked down at the signature. Kennedy switched his pen to his right hand and clicked it, causing the assistant chief to look up.

"You think you're so smart, don't you?" he growled. Spinning the pad back to Kennedy, he said, "Now do the same thing with your right hand."

The ruse worked. Kennedy was right-handed and had signed the will with it. But he was also cunning and knew this day could come. His mother had a saying, practice makes perfect. Kennedy knew that to be false. Practice only made better. He was glad he practiced writing with both hands. He shrugged and did his best to sign Harley Benton's name on the page. It was sloppy.

"So, can you tell me what this is all about?" Kennedy asked, still on the offensive.

"Let me ask you a few questions first. Did you have access to Harley Benton's office?"

"Detective Holmes," Kennedy began, making sure he called the Bulldog by his former job title, noticing the assistant chief flinch at the reference. "I worked hand in hand with Mr. Benton for over twenty years. I was his butler."

"You didn't answer my question. Did you, or did you not have access to Benton's office?"

Kennedy nodded. "Of course, I did. I fed him, cleaned up after him, and even ran his errands."

Now Bulldog smiled. "So, were you in his office the day he had the stroke?"

Kennedy knew he had to tread carefully. "I was."

"And what were you doing there?" The smile on Bulldog's face grew wider.

"Calling for an ambulance." He then added, "Under the circumstances, wouldn't that be your first task as well?"

The smile faded as Bulldog ignored the question by asking another. "Did you call anyone else?"

"Yes."

Bulldog awaited the answer. Kennedy stalled until the man asked the next question, delighting in the officer's frustration.

"TO WHOM?" Bulldog yelled.

"You don't have to get angry, detective. I'm here to answer any question you have." Although Kennedy was enjoying this discussion, he didn't want to overplay his hand.

Bulldog took his tone down a few notches. "With whom?"

"I called Mr. Benton's lawyer to inform him of the developments."

"Is that when you signed the will?" Bulldog asked innocently as if he was asking a simple question and not an incriminating one.

Kennedy was ready for him. "Sir, I did not sign anything. The lawyer told me to look for certain papers and to drop them at his office post haste. After the ambulance took Mr. Benton away, I did what I was told." *This will explain my fingerprints.*

The Bulldog scowled at his failed attempt at a confession. "Was there anyone else in the office with you?" he barked.

"No," the ex-butler lied. "Detective, will I be needing the services of a lawyer?"

Bulldog flinched. "It's assistant chief, NOT detective."

Kennedy's offensive had worked. He remained calm while the Bulldog was flustered.

"My apologies, *assistant* chief." Kennedy's emphasis on 'assistant' intentional.

The Bulldog scratched the back of his neck. "One last question. Where was Axel Ahearne when you were calling the ambulance?"

"I wasn't with him. I assume he stayed with Mr. Benton. That is where I left him. But I cannot be sure. You know what they say about assuming, don't you, detective?"

Exasperated, the Bulldog stood up and waved Kennedy to follow him. He interpreted the gesture to mean the assistant chief was well aware of the saying and by Kennedy's standards, it seemed this conversation had produced only one ass.

Will Ames was amazed at Benton's new ability to speak. He'd helped the old man with electronic stimulation of the left hand but that would not have returned Benton's speech. The old man had either recovered sooner than expected or had been fooling everyone all along.

Will wasn't sure which but was happy to be able to communicate. He also was unsure as to why Benton had made it clear that Will was the only one in the building to know about his improved condition.

Slipping into Benton's room he began to address the newly communicative patient.

"Well hello to you!" Will said cheerfully. "How are we feeling today?"

"Goot, Goot," answered Benton. Still unable to get the hard consonant sounds correctly, he began replacing D's with T's. Will thought it made him sound like a German in an old World War Two movie.

Another positive note was that movement was returning to his left arm. That development he could take credit for. When together there were no more tremors and his mobility was vastly improved. However, when someone other than Will was with him, the old man proved to be a highly skilled actor making certain his left arm remained limp.

"One thing bothers me. Why won't you let your doctors know about this?" he asked, pointing to his throat. "It's like a miracle. You should be shouting the news from the rooftops."

Considering the age and condition of the old man, Will revised his claim. "Well, I could shout for you."

Benton leaned forward. "Too soon," he claimed. "Unfinisht business. Have to be payshun." He pointed towards the desk drawer. Will opened it and produced the notepad and pen, handing them both to Benton.

The old man began to write and when finished, handed the notepad to Will, surprised to see the request.

"Can you tell me what this is all about?" Will asked.

"Nah yeht," responded the old man. "In time, son, in time."

"So, you want my mother to visit?"

Benton nodded his head.

"But you can't tell me why?"

This time the old man shook his head, again saying, "Nah yeht."

"But when? This is all very mysterious."

Benton sighed as he pointed at the desk drawer, a sign Will understood immediately. He tore the page and placed it in his pant pocket. The pad and pen he replaced in the drawer just as Hector poked his head in the door, motioning for Will to come out into the hallway. Once outside the door, he asked the orderly. "How's he doing?"

"I wish I could understand," Will replied. "I really do."

Hector put a hand on Will's shoulder. "We all do, Will, but God works in mysterious ways. On the other hand, we work according to the needs of our patients, so let's get back to work, shall we?"

Will could only surmise that Hector was talking about Harley Benton's silent condition. Little did Hector, or anyone else for that matter, realize as Will did that God's work and Benton's plan were both equally mysterious.

Winnie was desperate. She believed she could find Veronica by scouring the docket, the internet, the new list provided by Hector's friend at the abstract company, and even her intuition to come up with possible kidnapping sites. After an exhaustive search, she narrowed the list down to only three potential sites and called a cab. She knew each was a long shot but desperate times….

A cold rain continued to fall in the early evening darkness, so she grabbed an umbrella and ran towards her ride, the FALM parking lot lights showing her the way.

The first stop was an old mansion that a wealthy merchant had built in the late 1800s. It had been abandoned for some time now, run down and boarded up, a relic well past its prime. The Benton Falls Historical Society offered plans to city officials to restore it to its former glory, but each time the plan came up, Harley Benton found a way to have it defeated.

The petition to have it demolished passed through easily before Benton was incapacitated. Those plans were currently on hold, the restoration voices having grown louder now that political arms went untwisted and ears no longer whispered into by Harley Benton.

Winnie, a restoration supporter, felt the reason the old man was adamant about letting the place rot was narcissistic in nature, not wanting any refurbishing project to overshadow the best home in Benton Falls. His own Manor.

"Benton just wants to show off how big his junk is," she'd claim to the snickers of her fellow supporters.

As he parked in front of the mansion, the taxi driver said, "You know, you could have called an Uber." Winnie ignored him as she opened the cab door and took the wet steps up to the dilapidated mansion. "Clock is still ticking!" he yelled after her.

She closed her umbrella before stepping through the open entrance, the actual door having vanished long ago. The stench hit her in the face, making her turn her head to one side. Taking a handkerchief from her clutch, she covered her nose and mouth, subduing but not eliminating the foul odor.

"Veronica!" she called out before placing the handkerchief back to her face. Walking past what she deemed to be the parlor, she noticed small fiery glows from within. Wisps of smoke rose eerily in the air. "Crackheads," she whispered with contempt. *Kepner really is useless.*

"Veronica!" she yelled again. Still no answer. She stepped into the kitchen and looked around. Was there a cellar in this place? The urge to flee was only masked by her need to find Vee.

"Veron…" she began again but was interrupted by a growl.

"Would you shut up! There ain't no Veronica here. And if you were smart, you wouldn't be here either."

Standing behind her and blocking escape was a large man who wore a scruffy coat and torn pants. His hair was long and stringy, his beard full and unkempt, giving him the appearance of a large bear. His funky body odor added to the impression.

"I'm looking for my friend," Winnie said calmly, even though inside she felt a twinge of fear. "She's pregnant and needs my help."

"If you don't leave now," stated the bear man, "It'll be you looking for help. Unnerstand?"

"My good man, I'm here looking for my friend and I'm not leaving until either I find she's not here or if she is, comes home with me. Do you *unnerstand*?"

Growling, The bear man lunged at Winnie. She sidestepped him, planting the tip of her umbrella into his right foot while at the same time slapping him across the face with her clutch.

The beast fell to the ground writhing in pain and holding his injured foot. "Why'd ya do that?" he cried. Winnie's confidence grew as the bear man was now reduced to a mere cub.

"One shouldn't try and attack an old lady. Especially when she has weapons." She raised the umbrella once again, threatening the man's other foot.

"No, please! There is no Veronica here. I swear!" Heads from the crack parlor poked out in curiosity.

"Are you sure?" Winnie prodded.

"Of course. I swear!"

"Well, had you said this in the first place, we could have avoided this unpleasant little scene." She turned to walk away and as she passed the parlor, waved her umbrella at the heads, watching them duck back into the safety of their darkness and crack pipes.

"OK, Hazel, it's time to stop cleaning," chided Pinky. Pointing a thumb at Grizz, he added, "We need a third at cards, I'm tired of beating this big oaf and want to pick on you for a while." Pinky smiled widely as Grizz groused at his continued string of bad luck.

"Yeah, OK. Just let me finish this window." Veronica had cleaned half of the row of windows overlooking the interior of the building. Her bucket water turned a filthy grey from the dirt squeezed out of the sponge attached to the extender pole.

"There," she said. She put her hands on her hips admiring her handiwork. "Now we can get some decent light in here."

Both men looked up at her work. Just as she'd planned. She hoped they wouldn't need to look in that direction again.

"I gotta admit, you've spiffied this place up nice," said Grizz, forgetting about his card losses for a moment. "Real nice. Smells nice too."

Veronica half curtsied. It was the best she could do under her circumstances. "Why thank you, Grizz. I'm glad my efforts are appreciated."

"Pinky?" Grizz asked. "I'm hungry, are you?"

"Yeah, I could eat," Pinky replied. He got out of his seat and headed towards the refrigerator when Veronica stopped him.

"Oh no you don't. This is my kitchen now. Let me whip something up for you both. Go back to your cards and I'll have something ready shortly." She paused until they returned to the table before adding, "Let me just clean this mess up first."

She began by pouring the mucky water down the sink drain. Next, she took the wet sponge off the extender pole, placing it in the dish drainer to dry. Before her next task, she side-eyed the men. Convinced they were engrossed in their cards, she turned her back to them, pulled her drawing from its hiding place, and affixed it to the tip of the pole using a scrap piece as a loop. She then walked it over to the far end of the building, placing it in the corner. The white paper blending perfectly in with the white concrete wall. "I'll come back for you later," she whispered, before turning back toward the men.

She whistled while she assembled the necessary ingredients and began her meal prep, occasionally engaging the men in conversation. She wanted to keep them distracted until her final task was done.

"What are we having?" Grizz asked. "Whatever it is, it smells good!"

"You'll find out soon enough!" she teased.

She cooked as the men played. Once the lasagna was finished, she plopped a heaping portion onto their plates and brought them over to the table.

"There is plenty more for you guys, so eat up!"

One of the reasons she baked the dish was not only because it was delicious but had the property she desired. Men who ate a lot, especially at night, usually fell asleep early. It is said the way to a man's heart is through his stomach. Veronica didn't agree with that archaic musing. What she hoped for was that a way to a man's *circadian rhythm* was through his stomach to prove correct. She needed her men to fall asleep for her next task. Sleep that was long and deep.

After dinner, they played more gin rummy. Veronica watched as both men yawned incessantly. Grizz was the first to nod off. "Hey!" yelled Pinky. "Either finish the game or go to bed."

"Bed," responded Grizz as he got up and shuffled to his cot. Soon Veronica could hear muffled snoring.

To prompt Pinky, she faux yawned herself. "I'm bushed as well. Sleep tight," she said to the smaller man, who after turning off the lights, found his cot. It didn't take long for her to hear Pinky begin to snore as well.

Once she was sure they both had fallen asleep, she rolled out of bed, planting her feet firmly on the cold cement to steady herself. Early moonlight shone through the windows, guiding her way. *How fortunate.* Walking towards the far end of the building, she stopped at the sink and slowly opened a drawer to pick up a roll of clear tape. She proceeded to slink towards the extender pole in the corner when she heard Grizz ask, "Vee?" She contemplated ignoring him, but instead thought it better to answer.

"I have to pee," she whispered.

"Of course, you do," he grunted back before rolling over in his cot. It took a few moments before she heard him snore.

Now she had a dilemma. If he awoke again and she hadn't gone to the bathroom, he'd be suspicious. So, she redirected to the bathroom, did her business, and waited a little while longer.

To ensure she didn't make any noise, she didn't flush, leaving her urine as evidence, should they question her. It might not matter as she had to get up several times each night anyway, but she wasn't taking any chances. This mission was far too important.

After she felt she'd been in the bathroom long enough, she snuck out and headed over to the extender pole waiting for her. She affixed a piece of tape to the top and bottom of the drawing and checked to make sure the tip of the pole was in place under the loop, enough to stay put as long as she lifted the pole but liberate the drawing as she withdrew it.

Turning the release to extend the pole, she moved the extension to the right length before tightening it again. Hand over hand she raised the drawing until it reached window height. Pressing the paper to the window, she tapped it a bit too hard. Freezing, she waited for one or both men to catch her in the act. When neither did, she continued until the drawing was attached to the window with the tape.

Veronica took a breath hoping the tape would hold, before turning the release on the pole and slowly withdrawing the extension back in.

Stepping back, she placed the pole in the corner and looked up. In the moonlight, she could barely see the drawing. This was good. She only hoped the daylight obscured it as well.

She'd have to keep the men occupied with the last row of windows, a deflection long enough for someone to notice that there might be more in the building than just supplies and equipment.

"Next stop is the abandoned parts manufacturing plant out on Highway Twelve," Winnie instructed. This plant was owned by Benton and if there was ever a place to hide someone, this would be it. Benton's grandfather had built it during World War II hoping to cash in on wartime contracts. The end of the war and the small scale of parts manufactured sank the business.

Winnie had heard the rumors the place was haunted due to the number of those who tried to resurrect the plant and failed each time. And of course, the stories of ghostly encounters from people who spread those tales. Winnie, ever the pragmatist, believed the failures were from poor choices. The last one was in the 1970s due to stagflation.

The cab pulled into the access road and stopped at a gate with a metal chain across two posts. "This is as far as I go, ma'am," he said. Winnie exited the cab and began to walk toward the structure. The cabbie yelled after her, "Don't forget your protection!" Winnie went back and retrieved the umbrella, wondering if he meant protection from the rain or from whatever was inside.

It took some time but ultimately, she found a door that would open enough for her to squeeze through. Once inside, she knew why one would think the building was haunted. It was wide open flooring, vacant with all of the important machines and furniture removed years before. The only thing that filled it was darkness. Water dripped from the ceiling, forming puddles on the crusted and deteriorating concrete floor.

"Hello?" she yelled out. Her voice echoed in the cavernous building. "Veronica?"

Fear began to creep in but she doused it with her resolve to find Veronica. "I ain't 'fraid of no ghosts," she commented, stealing a line from the famous movie. "But just in case…" Winnie lifted the point of her umbrella out in front as a precaution.

From time to time, she called out as she walked through the building, the only responses coming from the echo. She climbed up a flight of stairs to the offices above. The structure was designed to have the manufacturing on the ground floor and the management above so the bosses could watch over their minions' progress. Darkness filled the windowless offices, the electricity needed for lights, shut off long ago.

"Veronica?" she said, this time whispering.

A clang broke the silence behind her coming from the manufacturing floor. Turning towards the stairs she cautiously made her way toward the noise, hoping this would lead her to the poor girl.

Another creaking sound like metal on metal came from the other side of the building causing her to cringe, yet she moved toward it slowly. She moved along the wall of the building and crept towards the noise, making none of her own until she could determine what or who had caused it.

Stopping to press herself flat against the wall, she heard footsteps splashing in the water as they passed her. Winnie deduced her kidnapped friend would not have the freedom to walk around the place unescorted. Plus, the heavy footsteps were definitely masculine. Deciding it was time to leave, she inched her way back toward the entrance, the door still slightly ajar, the dim outside light showing the way.

Winnie was just about to slip through when a hand grabbed her shoulder. Instinctively, she swung her umbrella in the direction of the grabber, smashing it against the wall, missing the assailant. She once again tried to escape when the hand grabbed her arm. She tried to stab the assailant with the umbrella, but it was taken from her hand. She did the only thing she could think of. She backed out into the rain and screamed.

"Lady! Shhhh! It's just me!" said the cabbie, her broken umbrella in his right hand. "I was worried about ya!"

Winnie stopped screaming and punched the cabbie in the arm. "What are you doing scaring an old lady like that? I could have had a heart attack!"

"I was just checking up on you," he said sheepishly. "Didn't mean to scare ya."

Winnie put her hands on her knees and tried to catch her breath. "Jesus, Mary, and Joseph," she exhaled.

The cabbie rubbed his arm and finished the phrase, "And all the bald-headed angels."

Winnie looked up at him in disbelief.

"What?" he replied. "My grandmother used to say that whenever she got frustrated with my gramps." He helped Winnie up and escorted her to the cab, both getting rain-soaked. Once there, the now useless umbrella was tossed into the back seat.

As the cabbie settled into the driver's seat, Winnie said, "One more stop."

"Haven't you had enough tonight? If you don't have a heart attack, you'll probably catch your death of pneumonia."

"Oh, now you're a doctor practicing medicine out of your cab?" she snapped. Noticing the hurt look in his eyes through the rearview mirror, she apologized. "You don't understand. My girl is out there and in trouble. And she's pregnant! I *have* to find her."

The cabbie nodded and took the directions. He began to drive, the windshield wipers sloshing away the rain. On the outside of town, they came upon a modest ranch with a covered porch overlooking a nice-sized lawn. On one side was a small forest. On the other, what was left of a harvested cornfield, its withered husks waving in the wind like faded skeletons. A remnant of yellow police tape attached itself to one husk causing it to flutter like an airfield windsock. A for sale sign was planted on the front lawn indicating the former owner would never reside there again. Or able to kill or hurt anyone. Ever.

This house belonged to the person who had murdered residents at the FALM. Including Leif.

The Hastener.

"Whoa," said the cabby. "If I had known you wanted to come to the house of a whacko killer, I wouldn't have made the drive."

"Relax, that person tried to kill me, not you. And now locked up in the Psych Center and can't harm either of us, so let's just check it out and be on our way." Winnie didn't want to be here any more than the cab driver but she had to make damn sure neither was Veronica.

They both exited the cab and with the rain in their faces, walked around the house looking for signs of life. When they found none, Winnie stepped up on the porch and tried the front door. It was locked, the lockbox holding the key hung around the doorknob, indicating a realtor had been on-premise showing the home. Winnie wondered if the deeds of the previous owner were disclosed to prospective buyers.

"You don't actually want to go in anyway, right?" asked the cabbie. Winnie, satisfied no one was there, shook her head. She'd had enough of the murderous wretch. She didn't want to complicate things with a breaking and entering charge as well.

As the cabbie drove her back to the FALM, Winnie felt defeated. The first two locations made sense because they each had a connection to Harley Benton. The third location was just a fishing expedition.

Now she was out in this storm but had caught nothing but perhaps a cold. She had to stop guessing and come up with a different way, no, *better* way to find Veronica. Fishing was no longer a viable option.

Little did Winnie know at the time those fishing for *her*, would soon come to visit.

# Chapter Ten

"Sorry Vee, we'll have to tie you up. We gotta errand to run," Grizz said, pointing to her chair. He had begun calling her this shortened version recently. She didn't mind, thinking her plan was working. It didn't hurt to think that the familiarity could also save her life. When you become human to your captors, it's harder for them to… well, that was a thought for down the road.

Right now, she needed to play along.

"Sure, I understand, Grizz. You got a job to do." She paused before asking, "Where to today?" She hoped to get a small kernel of intel. It didn't work as Grizz wore a darkened expression. Pinky jumped in, "Never you mind where we're going. We got an appointment is all."

This morning, both were summoned to the second floor by the old man. They whispered so she couldn't hear well. When they returned, both were in buoyant moods. She wondered who they were meeting, but she got a clue when she heard one say to the other, "Gotta get her today. So, no messin' up."

*Her.*

Veronica surmised they received permission from the old man and knew who they were 'going to get.' Fear struck her hard. *If only there was some way to warn Winnie, but how?*

Grizz finished tying her to the chair and asked, "Do you have to go to the bathroom?"

"A little late for that, don't you think," she responded, looking down at the rope that bound her.

"Sorry, got ahead of myself." Grizz took a strip of duct tape and placed it gingerly over her mouth smoothing it across her cheeks. "Sorry, but strict orders from upstairs." Rather than muffle a complaint, she tilted her head and raised her eyebrows with a look that meant, "Eh, what are you gonna do?"

"C'mon Grizz, we're gonna be late for our 'appointment.'" Pinky used air quotes when he pronounced the last word, solidifying Veronica's fear Winnie was the intended engagement.

The two thugs left her, the metal door clanging shut behind them. She felt being alone was worse than having the company of two men who planned her kidnapping and possibly a second. She wriggled to see if she could escape the bonds but to no avail. Fatigue set in, her chin resting on her chest. The only thing left to do was nap. And await her captor's return.

⁓

Axel walked up to the station desk and announced himself. "I'm here to pick up Mr. Kennedy, please?" Axel still didn't know his friend's first name and felt shame he hadn't found out.

The officer went down a list. "Kennedy…hmmm. Oh, here it is. Brogan Kennedy."

"Brogan?" whispered Axel. *Where did that odd name come from?*

The police officer waved for Axel to sit down across from the desk. Kennedy came out a door with Assistant Chief Holmes behind him. The Bulldog looked sour.

"How are you doing?" Axel asked, ignoring the ex-detective.

Kennedy shrugged his shoulders, answering, "As well as to be expected. The accommodations are not exactly the Ritz, but it was comfortable and Detective Holmes was very considerate."

Axel hid a smile at the wrong title reference. The Bulldog just scowled.

As the two walked out the door, Kennedy put a finger to his lips. Axel didn't say another word until they were inside the car and driving.

"Is this about the will?" Axel asked.

Kennedy nodded. "It would seem someone tipped off the police claiming the old man did not sign the will. That put the suspicion right on my back."

"But no one really can prove it, can they?" Axel felt perspiration under his arms.

Kennedy responded, "I think not. A handwriting expert may be able to claim the signature is fake, but not who wrote it. If you are asked two questions, these need to be your answers: First, were you in Benton's office at any time the day he had his stroke?"

Axel jumped in with his answer, "Of course I was. We were burning those awful pictures used to blackmail folks."

"My dear boy, I have always been upfront with you. I will remain so. But this one time and hopefully it's the only time, I will ask you to lie. You were NOT in the office with me as I called the ambulance. You were with Mr. Benton. Correct?"

Axel took a deep breath. "If you think it necessary."

"To protect you, yes. And did you leave the room for any reason?"

Axel thought for a moment. That day was embedded in his memory. "Yes."

"All right then. So where did you go?"

Axel nodded his head in understanding. "I went to check to see if the ambulance had arrived."

"Good, because I told the police I assumed you were with Benton. But you never came into his office. So, stick with that story and you'll be all right."

As Axel drove, he asked, "What's the second question?"

"Why are your fingerprints on Benton's will?" Kennedy responded.

"Mr. Benton gave me control over his estate. The lawyer Grange made me read it."

"Another good answer."

The two men rode in silence before Axel broke it. "Look, I want you to know if the police gather enough proof to convict, then I'll step up…"

Kennedy leaned forward, interrupting Axel. "No. You have no part in this. I have done some dishonorable things in my life and need to accept whatever verdict comes down, but I will not have you involved in this fray. It is my fight and mine alone. I've already done enough damage to you and if need be, will take the punishment I so richly deserve. I'll not hear another word. Now stick to the plan, understand?"

Axel nodded his head. He decided to lighten the mood. "So, *Brogan,* How does it feel to be out of the hoosegow?"

Kennedy flinched. "It was my grandfather's name and was passed down to me."

"But you don't use it. Are you not proud of your grandfather?"

"Master Axel, before you go any further, my grandfather was an upstanding and honorable man. Worked hard his whole life and took great care of his family. Make no mistake, I am very proud of the man and my relationship with him." Kennedy stopped there but Axel prodded for more.

"So why not use the name to honor the man?"

Kennedy bowed his head and replied softly, "Because I'm not worthy." He looked up at Axel, his expression pleading. "So let us never use that name again, shall we?"

Axel's attempt at humor had failed, the ensuing silence uncomfortable between them. He drove on focused on the road until Kennedy asked, nonchalantly, "By the way, later that fateful day in the kitchen, how did you like the sandwich I made for you?"

"It was…." Axel stopped short, realizing the ploy. "What sandwich?"

"Good. Very good." Kennedy sat back, confident in his plan to protect his friend. It turned out Axel could indeed lie and do it so well.

Winnie was at her desk when Dottie called. "Miss Winnie, there are two gentlemen here who would like to see you. I told them you were finishing a meeting. I'll sit them down and make them comfortable until you are ready."

Winnie found Dottie's comments odd. The receptionist usually took her lead on visitors, deferring to her boss, but this message showed Dottie taking the lead. Winnie looked at the security feeds Hector had installed and clicked on the view of the front desk. There were two men, one tall and one short. She recognized neither.

She wasn't expecting anyone this morning. Perhaps they were inquiring about an elderly relative. Or maybe they were detectives. Her suspicious nature kicked into overdrive recalling the ransom note claiming to have kidnapped her. She was determined to remain cautious.

Winnie walked out to the front and greeted her new guests. "Gentlemen, I don't have anyone on my calendar this morning. Is there something I can do for you?"

Both men looked at each other in what Winnie could only describe as concern. *Strange.* Walking to the door, she noticed a car sitting in the circular drive. It was a black sedan. "Is that your car parked out front?"

The smaller man nodded. "Is that a problem?" The tone was menacing.

"First of all, there are signs out there. That space is for the elderly to get dropped off or picked up, so yes. It is a problem."

"Oh, my bad," said the larger one. He got up but the smaller man put a hand on his arm and pulled him back into the seat.

"Your car is also running," Winnie commented. *Something is not right. These guys sound familiar, but I can't place them.*

"Well, we don't plan on staying here long. We have a busy schedule today so if you don't mind," the smaller man said. He stood up and introduced himself as Robert Plant. "I'd like to discuss if this is a good place to put…err… if this home would be a good fit for my mom?"

Winnie hid a smile. Robert Plant. *Is the big guy going to introduce himself as John Lennon?*

"If we could go to your office and discuss this, I'd appreciate it," offered Mr. Plant. "Some place quiet. As I said, we have a busy day ahead."

Winnie thought quickly. "We usually have our marketing director handle new prospective residents. Dottie, could you set up an appointment with Betty?" She tipped her head to one side and raised an eyebrow when Dottie gave her a quizzical look. The position of marketing director had yet to be filled and as far as Dottie knew, there was no one by the name of Betty who worked at the FALM.

Before Winnie turned back to the gentlemen, she winked at Dottie.

"Oh, sure," Dottie replied, once getting the point. Winnie could play the fake name game, too.

"Well send another bullet and kill poor buck," complained Mr. Plant. "I must insist you handle this. She's our mother and all. You know how it is."

*Good God!* Winnie froze at the odd saying. These guys didn't want to talk about their mother. And they certainly weren't detectives. Recalling the conversation overheard in the grocery store, it wasn't hard to put two and two together. A pregnant girl with the same cravings as Veronica? The same absurd saying about bullets and killing poor buck? Yes, these two were certainly the same fellows from the grocery store. Being here now was no coincidence. And with a car idling in front of the building, the math added up, equaling a pair of thugs whose intentions could only mean one thing…danger.

Regaining her composure, Winnie asked, "How old is Mrs. Plant?"

"Who?" replied the big man, only to get elbowed by the smaller man before answering.

"Eighty-seven. Mom's eighty-seven."

"This is highly irregular," Winnie explained, "But if you give us a moment, I'm sure we can accommodate you." Winnie stepped over to Dottie's desk.

"You're not actually thinking…" Dottie whispered, tilting her head to keep an eye on the strangers in her lobby. She must have felt the danger as well.

"Of course not," Winnie whispered back. "They aren't here on that kind of business." Dottie looked worried. "Do you want me to call the police?"

Winnie shook her head. "Not the police when we have someone on premises. I have a better idea. Do you have an intake form available?"

Dottie looked in her desk where she pulled out a sheet of paper and attached it to a clipboard.

"Good. Now have them fill this out and I'll call you so we can reschedule." Dottie gave Winnie a look of concern. "Now don't you worry. These guys are like foxes in the hen house where only two things can happen. One, they won't find this hen in her office."

Dottie cocked her head at the reference in understanding. "And two?" she whispered.

"That's the best part. Once you've rescheduled, the foxes have only one place to go…*Their* den."

Dottie patted Winnie's hand as if to wish her luck.

"Gentlemen," Winnie said, addressing the two thugs she now believed were not there to input an old lady but to extricate one. "Dottie here will take your information and I'll see you in my office shortly." This seemed to appease both men.

"Wait for my call," Winnie whispered to Dottie.

Once in her office, she called Hector and told him to go to the front desk. Then she quickly picked up her cell phone and pulled the Tag-it! from her pocket. Slipping out of her office, she left through the back door and around to the front. She slid across the building until she came up to the black sedan, its engine still running. The only reason to keep a car running at an assisted living facility was nothing if not nefarious. Smiling, she sidled up to the car on the driver's side so the sedan would block the vision of the two men inside. Opening the back door, she slid the Tag-It! into the mesh cargo net on the back of the driver seat and closed the door.

There was only one way to find out if these two were holding Veronica. If not, she had another KIT to plant. Given what she had learned, she didn't believe she would need it. Heading back to her office, she called Dottie from her cell.

"Please apologize to the gentlemen for me, I had to leave for an important engagement, but they should set up an appointment for tomorrow. Make it in the afternoon. Don't worry if they give you any trouble, I called Hector. He's on his way."

Hanging up, she entered her office and watched the monitor of the lobby to see how the two men reacted. She was not disappointed.

"I insist we see her right now!" the small man barked.

"Yeah, now," added the larger one. He leaned over the desk, his face almost touching Dottie's.

"Is there a problem here?" asked the security officer. Hector had arrived right on time.

"Oh, nooo," stated Dottie calmly as she stared down Grizz. He retreated. "These gentlemen set an appointment to see Winnie tomorrow afternoon. About their *mother*."

"I see," replied Hector. "I'm sure you'll find this to be a first-rate home for your mom. Safe and secure."

"Thank you for visiting us, gentlemen. So, we'll see you tomorrow?" Dottie smiled sweetly, "I have you down for two p.m. sharp!"

Winnie saw this as a cue for them to leave so she snuck back outside and stood by the corner of the building watching the two men exit in a rush. The small one was swearing. They both jumped into the sedan and left the parking lot.

Winnie wasn't available today and would make damn sure she wouldn't be available tomorrow either. But she did have a plan. Tomorrow, she had a very special appointment to attend to. As she watched the green dot on her phone course its way forward toward the fox's den, she smiled at her deception. "Tag, you're it," she whispered.

Jules pulled up, a suspicious eye trained on the old woman. Through the open passenger side window she asked, "Winnie, what are you doing?"

"Jules dear, I'm glad you came by. I only have a minut… Wait, did Axel tell you to keep an eye on me?"

Jules looked sheepishly at the steering wheel and answered, "Those were his exact words."

"I knew it. Doesn't think we're up to the challenge to find our girl, is he? When you think about it, he's keeping you out of trouble as well."

"He said that too. Men are so blind, aren't they?"

"And then the blind men shall see," said Winnie. "But not until we women turn on the lights."

Jules began to protest. "I don't think it…" She stopped and just shook her head.

"I'm not one for sitting around," Winnie said. "Especially for men who aren't as good as we are for this task at hand. I have an idea and I'm going to need your help."

Jules, clearly on team Winnie, responded. "I'm all ears."

The old woman glanced at her phone. "Keep the car running, I'll be right back," she said, sprinting through the front door.

Reaching the front desk, she addressed her receptionist. "Dottie, you know the plan for those two men. Tomorrow afternoon, please take them to my office, sit them down, and give them coffee. Make sure you let them know I'll be with them shortly but whatever you do, do not let them leave my office. Understood?"

Dottie cocked her head to the side and looked over her glasses at Winnie. "How long should I keep them?"

Winnie grinned and said, "Until I call you and have you reschedule our meeting…again."

"They're as good as detained," Dottie yelled after Winnie as she sprinted out the front door, and then jumped into Jules's car.

"Winnie, how can a woman of your age be so spry? And fearless?" Jules asked.

Winnie, breathing heavily, responded, "Good genes, I guess. And good Irish whiskey. Now drive!"

"Wait, Winnie, where are we going? Axel said I had to…."

"I know what he said. 'Keep an eye on her.' He didn't say where so you drive and I'll be right next to you, so you can keep an eye on me." She told Jules about the two men in the grocery store, and how they came to visit her at the FALM. She also told her about the Tag-It! she had hidden in their car.

"Hopefully, it will lead us to our girl." She finished by showing Jules her phone and pointed to the moving green dot they were now chasing. "Eyes on the road," she commanded. "Don't need to end up in the hospital."

Jules stifled a grin at Winnie's contradictory instructions.

"This was dangerous stuff they were going to attempt," Winnie explained. "But we're craftier than they are."

"Axel wants us out of the hunt," said Jules. "Should we even be doing this?"

The old woman snapped back. "Dearie, he doesn't even know where the den is. My plan is solid and after his condescending attitude towards the women in his life, you included, I find I don't much care what Axel thinks."

Winnie continued her navigation while Jules drove. They came up to a large parking lot in front of a construction site. A tall skeleton of metal beams stretched several stories into the sky, heavy equipment moved earth and building materials, and the air filled with the sounds of construction.

The place was filled with men in hard hats reminding Winnie of the small construction puppets from a favorite TV program of years past. "Doozers," she whispered.

Planted in the front of the structure was a sign that read, "New home of Grandview Heights, a mixed-use oasis." The sentence below read, "For leasing information contact the sales office." A red arrow pointed to a trailer at the side of the building.

Confused, she looked again at her phone. This was the address the Tag-it! had shown her, the green dot stationary.

"This can't be right, can it?" Jules asked. This construction site was just north of the downtown area where there used to be a smelting furnace. The area was aptly named Furnaceville, but the concept planners probably felt that was a poor marketing choice, thus changing the name.

"Doesn't look right to me, either. Too much traffic, too many people, and no closed space to hide anyone. But look."

Winnie held her phone up so Jules could see the green dot blipping right in front of them.

Jules scratched her chin. "Is it possible these guys just stopped in here on their way to the hideout?"

"Possible," replied Winnie. "But why? Maybe their boss works here or they've come to collect money from someone."

"So, you think these guys are not only kidnappers but loan sharks as well?"

Winnie shrugged her shoulders.

Jules went on. "Winnie, you might be watching too many gangster films. I'm not sure why they're here but one other possibility exists."

"And that is?" Winnie asked.

"The possibility these guys are not your kidnappers. If they were, this would have to be the right site in plain sight. Furthermore, where is the black sedan?"

The clues did put these guys as potential suspects, Winnie was certain. But this location just didn't make sense. But then again, nothing about this situation made sense. She made a mental note to ask Hector to call his friend at the whatchamacallit company to investigate the owners of the building and construction company. *Oh yea, Abstract.*

The two women drove back to the FALM in silence, both caught up in their own thoughts.

"What's the next move," asked Jules.

"Wait a second." Winnie had an idea. "A short while ago you said, 'the right site in plain sight.' Are you available tomorrow afternoon around one thirty?" Jules nodded.

"Then pick me up at the FALM because I have a hunch you might be on to something."

"A hunch?" Jules looked perplexed. "About what?"

"Hiding in plain sight and Doozers, dear. Doozers."

Axel was stumped. He and Kennedy believed they had thought of everything. They searched records, spoke with real estate agents, and even drove all over town scoping the best places to hide a kidnapped pregnant woman, all to no avail. Perhaps Winnie was right after all. They needed to think in new ways. He wished his brother Leif was here. Leif had a penchant for the dark side and even though Axel hesitated at the thought, believed if anyone could think like a criminal, it would be his brother. But Leif *wasn't* here. The irony that his wayward brother turned himself into a hero didn't escape him. Even in death, Leif seemed to be mocking his younger sibling.

"Who sends a ransom note and then fails to follow up?" asked a weary Axel. No one had heard back from the kidnappers and both men were worried that could mean bad news for their pregnant friend.

"What about the ledger from Benton's office?" asked Axel. "Maybe there is someone who's holding a grudge against the old man?" The ledger in question was a blackmail tool Benton used against his enemies and friends alike. Both Axel and Kennedy showed repugnance toward such tactics but both agreed that Benton was using it as insurance to get what he needed.

"The cost of doing bad business," Kennedy had argued.

"You still have it, right?"

Kennedy cocked his head. "The original is with Kepner, remember?"

Axel looked suspiciously at his friend. "But?"

Kennedy chuckled. "But, we also need a good insurance policy, don't you think?"

Axel blushed at the thought that to stay out of trouble for not reacting quickly enough to help Benton after his stroke, they had to resort to something both unethical and illegal. *Two wrongs don't make a right,* came to mind.

Kennedy went over to Veronica's piano and opened the top. He reached in and fumbled around until he found what he was looking for. Pulling his arm out, Axel saw he held a stack of papers held together with a large clip. "Pages I *didn't* give to Kepner," Kennedy said, waving the insurance policy at Axel. "Dumb police couldn't find the ransom note so I figured they wouldn't find these either."

Axel began to pour over the pages from the ledger as Kennedy peered over his shoulder.

"How about…?" Axel began, pointing to a name. Kennedy shut him down almost immediately. "Nope. He's in prison. Tax evasion, remember?"

Axel nodded. Running a finger down more names, he stopped again. Turning to Kennedy, the ex-butler shook his head. "He passed away a few months ago. I have to keep an eye on everyone on this list. You never know when someone will try to make trouble."

Axel went back to the ledger, again running a finger down the list of names. He stopped at a pair of initials. "Do you know who this is?"

Kennedy looked down. "AF?" He scratched his head as he thought. "There are a few I couldn't account for and this was one of them. But look, It's not a payment to Benton, it's a payment to AF."

Axel tapped his chin in thought. "Wait a second, wasn't this one of the payments we stopped when we took over?"

"Yes. You are correct. The check was always made out to cash so we couldn't figure out why he was paying this person or who it was. If it was important to them, they would have come forward, yet no one has."

"Grange told me the reason the old man never used electronic transfers was because he was old fashioned and didn't trust the internet. But I'm guessing he wanted to keep these payments secret. But for what?"

Kennedy shrugged and then pointed to a number on the page. "Do we know what 212 stands for next to the payment?"

Axel thought for a moment. "The beginning of a phone number? Address? No, it's gotta be a post office box!"

Kennedy nodded. "I think you're right. The postal workers won't give us the name of the person who owns the box, but it doesn't mean we can't scope it out and see if anyone shows up, does it?"

They devised a plan to take turns watching the post office for signs of the box holder. This plan included not getting caught. They were under suspicion of forgery; neither man wanted to add stalking to the list of potential crimes.

Axel's phone rang. It was the lawyer, Harold Grange. After he hung up, he turned to Kennedy. "Guess we have to wait on the Hardy Boys mystery stakeout. The lawyer requests our presence in his office tomorrow afternoon."

The next day, Harold Grange, the lawyer overseeing Harley Benton's estate, sat at his desk, and looked over it at the people present for the meeting. Kennedy and Axel sat in chairs to his right while Kepner, on behalf of the police department, was seated to his left.

"Gentlemen, this meeting has been called to discuss the allegations of impropriety concerning Mr. Harley Benton's will and its legitimacy. It has been alleged the signature on this document is not that of Mr. Benton, but a forgery." Grange held up the document for all to see.

Looking over at the chief of police, Axel spoke up, "Do we need our lawyer present?" Although Grange assisted Axel on behalf of Benton, representing him on this particular issue would be a conflict of interest.

Lawyer Grange put a hand up. "This isn't a court of law. Today's meeting is to discuss the viability of you continuing to represent the estate of Harley Benton. You have every right to an attorney, but at this point, we're just looking for a few answers. Due diligence if you will." Grange waited for a response but Axel went silent. The lawyer began again.

"Mr. Kennedy, you had access to Mr. Benton's office, and weren't you the one who found the will at my direction?"

Kennedy stood up, "I did and I was sir." His answer was short and to the point. No need to tell people how to build a watch when all they wanted to know was the time.

Grange waved for Kennedy to sit. "It's not necessary to stand." Looking at the document he asked the ex-butler, "Before bringing it to my office, did you forge your ex-employer's signature on this document?"

Again, Kennedy's answer was brief, if untruthful. "No."

Grange addressed Axel. "Mr. Ahearne, did you forge Mr. Benton's signature on this document?"

Following Kennedy's lead, his answer was also brief. "No."

"Did you," Grange continued, "see anyone else sign this document?" Axel looked at the stoic Kennedy before answering in the negative.

Turning his attention to Police Chief Kepner, the lawyer asked, "Chief, what were the findings of your investigation into the potential forgery?"

Kepner cleared his throat. "Like you, I received an anonymous call stating the document was forged. I had a handwriting analysis done on the signature. It had most of the markings of Benton's with a few discrepancies but the expert's finding was inconclusive. He could not prove one way or the other if was indeed a forgery. Lastly, I had both Mr. Kennedy and Mr. Ahearne submit to a signature test which was also inconclusive. He doubted either of the gentlemen seated next to me could have successfully copied Mr. Benton's signature accurately."

"But he couldn't rule it out, either?"

Kepner nodded. "That is correct."

Grange asked the final question, "Will there be any further investigations into this alleged forgery?"

Kepner adjusted in his seat. "No sir. The lack of evidence doesn't warrant it. The only way we'd consider reopening the investigation is if Benton himself were to come forward and testify it was not his signature. Given his circumstances, we all know that is an unlikely scenario. Therefore, this investigation has come to an end."

Grange adjusted his glasses. "Very well, then I see no reason to make any changes to the arrangement Mr. Benton put into place before his medical issues appeared. Mr. Ahearne, you will remain in control of the Benton estate."

The three men stood up. Kennedy and Axel shook hands and then turned towards the door. Grange's desk phone rang and he picked it up. "Yes?" he said. "What? Are you sure? Well, of course, let them in." He hung up the phone and addressed the men. "Gentlemen don't leave yet. It seems as though we have one more witness to speak with. And Chief Kepner, hold off on discontinuing the investigation. It seems as if the unlikely… well, isn't."

All eyes went to the door as Harley Benton was wheeled through by Will, followed by a man no one recognized.

"Mr. Benton, so glad to have you out and about!" gushed Grange. "Please, come up to the desk and get comfortable." Looking at Will, he asked, "Can I get anything for him?"

"No," barked Benton. "Ain't ted yet." He shot a nasty look towards Kennedy and Axel.

Will translated, "Mr. Benton has regained some of his speech and wants me to inform you all that he is not dead yet. On the contrary."

Axel and Kennedy exchanged worried glances. *Benton could talk?*

The gentleman behind Will handed him a large envelope who, in turn, handed over to Grange. The lawyer looked over the document and recognition appeared across his face.

Addressing Benton, Grange asked, "Is it your wish to sign this to replace *this*?" He held up the new envelope and then the document under forgery scrutiny.

"Yeth," Benton answered. His answer was clearly understood.

Grange turned towards the two men who had been handling Benton's affairs. "Gents, it seems we won't need to look any further into this old will. Mr. Benton will be replacing it with this new one."

"Wait a second," interrupted Axel. "The original will states in case of death or incapacitation. We should get a medical opinion to make sure Mr. Benton is of sound mind!"

The gentleman behind Will handed him a new envelope. Will placed it in Grange's hand. "This will suffice. It's from his doctor." Grange pulled out a sheet of paper and read it to himself.

Axel interrupted again, "How do we know this doctor is reputable?"

Grange looked over his glasses and turned the sheet of paper towards Axel. It was on FALM letterhead. "Reputable enough?"

Axel was about to add to his complaint when Kennedy stopped him by patting his arm, before commenting himself. "We still need to witness his signature to make sure it's legitimate. AND a notary to sign off."

The man behind Will had not spoken up until this point. He addressed Grange. "Your secretary is a public notary, is she not?"

"Why yes, she is. If that's all right with you, Mr. Benton." Harley nodded his head. "Good," stated Grange. Motioning for Will to move Benton closer to his desk, the lawyer placed the document in front of the old man for his signature. He then called his secretary to join them. "And bring your stamp."

Once all the paperwork was completed, Grange dismissed the three original men. "Mr. Ahearne, you are relieved of your duty as overseer of the Benton Estate."

"Wait," interrupted Axel. "What does relieved mean?"

Grange lifted the new will and spoke, "According to this new document, all finances, property, businesses, and everything belonging to Mr. Benton and overseen by you is now once again his personal property. So, you are no longer in control of his estate."

Axel looked forlornly at Kennedy who shook his head.

"What about Winnie?" asked Axel. "She's the general manager at the FALM."

"Oww," said Benton scowling, his contempt evident.

Will translated, "That is out. As in fired. Effective immediately."

"Mr. Benton is this your intention?" asked Grange, wanting the translation to be clear.

Benton nodded his head. A sly grin formed as he whispered to Will. As the young man went to Grange's desk, he retrieved the disputed will, no longer necessary to file in the lawyer's office. Benton took the document and handed it to the new person, who placed it in a soft briefcase. The old man turned his gaze toward Kennedy and lifted his right hand in the shape of a gun, like a kid playing cops and robbers. He fired the pretend gun at Kennedy with a look so malevolent, even the stoic ex-butler felt the fear of what it meant: *You're next.*

The act went unnoticed by Grange as he closed the meeting. "Well, gentlemen, this concludes our business here today so you are free to leave. Mr. Benton and I have some business to discuss."

"That won't be necessary," said the man behind Will. "We'll take our leave also." Will grabbed the back of Benton's wheelchair and turned it towards the door.

Grange looked stricken. "But Mr. Benton, there's the matter of setting things back to before your, umm, condition worsened."

"Again, unnecessary," said the man.

"Well, you've seemed to think of everything, haven't you?" asked a rattled Grange. "Just who are you anyway?"

"My name is Carlton Flack and I'm his new lawyer," came the response. Then turning towards the chief, stated, "Furthermore, on behalf of Mr. Benton, we'll be making a complaint against these two men." Flack waved a hand at Axel and Kennedy. "For forgery."

"Mr. Benton?" Grange pleaded. Benton put a hand in the air and motioned for Will to turn him around, facing Grange.

Pointing a gnarled finger at Grange, Benton began to speak. "You. Are. Fired," said the old man slowly. This time there was no need for translation.

With their release from running the Benton Foundation, Kennedy and Axel had more than enough time to monitor the post office. They had just arrived, sitting silently in the parking lot watching as people entered and departed. The two men also had plenty of time to worry over the threat imposed by Harley Benton's new lawyer.

Axel broke the silence. "What are we gonna do?" He wasn't just scared, he was petrified. Axel had never run afoul of the law before. Not even a parking ticket.

"We," Kennedy began, his usual calmness did nothing to appease Axel's fear, "aren't going to do anything. You are not involved in the deception. You were not even in the room, right?"

"If you say so." Axel fidgeted with the ring containing Leif's ashes. "But I can't let you take the rap alone. There has to be a way to stop Benton's lawyer."

"Axel, there are two things to consider. Remember when I took Benton's key from his robe pocket? After he'd had the stroke?"

"Yeah, but what…"

Kennedy interrupted. "He watched me do it. So, he knows *I* went into his office."

"That doesn't prove you forged his signature."

"No, it doesn't. But it's proof enough that I *could* have. You, on the other hand, stay out of it. I might get arrested, but there is absolutely no proof to implicate you in the process. You let me worry about Benton."

"So, what's the other thing? You said 'two' things to consider."

Kennedy sighed. "Have you forgotten our friend Veronica has been kidnapped?"

A chastised Axel bowed his head. "No."

"Good, then let's get back to the task of finding her. Hand me the binoculars, please."

Axel did as he was told. Their plan was simple. From their car, they watched through binoculars to find ordinary people arriving with letters and boxes, to buy stamps, or pick up their mail. But so far, they had seen no one attempting to open box number 212.

Kennedy had an idea for Axel as he watched. "Why don't you go ask the postal worker if you can rent a box and ask specifically for 212? Say it's special for some reason. When they tell you it's taken, maybe you can gather some intel on it. Or at least see if you can leave a message to ask for it from the box holder."

"You really think that's going to work?" Axel asked, the skepticism obvious. "I just hope we don't get caught. Can you imagine what Winnie would say if she knew what we were doing?"

Kennedy laughed at the thought. No one ever knew what would come spewing from the old lady, but one thing was for sure, it wouldn't be good. Still, the two men had to do something. Time was running out and so far, this was their only strong lead.

"I feel like a private dick in those old movies," Axel said, as he got out of the car.

Kennedy smirked. "If the gumshoe fits."

Axel wasn't sure what he meant by that, the age difference between the two seemed sometimes so vast, that Axel didn't understand most of the phrases Kennedy uttered.

"Whatever," he responded as he walked towards the post office. "Gumshoe," he said aimlessly, vowing to look up the definition when he had a moment to do so.

Opening the door, he met a woman coming out. As Winnie had taught him, he stepped back and waved a hand in a sweeping gesture of chivalry. "After you," he said, letting the woman leave, before walking into the lobby. There was a longer line than he expected but fifteen minutes later, he stood in front of the postal worker, who asked, "Box 212 you say?"

Axel answered, "Yes, it was my box number growing up. We lived right near a post office and I'd like to have the same number. Reminds me of home. If it's not available…"

"Well, you're in luck. Someone just canceled box number 212. It's all yours."

Axel stepped back. "What do you mean, 'just?'"

"The past box holder just canceled a short while ago."

"What? But I didn't see…." Axel stopped himself. The postal worker didn't know he'd been spied upon and Axel wanted to keep it that way. "You said a short while ago?"

"Yeah, lemme see, here's the form, and once you've…"

"Did you get a good look at who it was?"

"Umm, some lady with brown hair but that's all I remember. Now if you fill out this form and…"

Axel never heard the rest of the instructions as he sped out the door searching for the woman for whom he had courteously opened the door. He wouldn't find her. Frustrated, Axel got back into the car to tell Kennedy the bad news.

"You're kidding me?" asked Kennedy.

"Can't make this up. Now what?"

The two men sat in thought contemplating their next move. To make light of a bad situation, Kennedy joked. "Well, it looks like this gumshoe got stuck."

Axel didn't laugh. He still didn't know what Kennedy meant. But whatever the ex-butler was referring to, Axel felt they should get unstuck. And soon. Veronica's well-being depended upon it.

⁓

Grizz was getting tired of this gig. Sitting around playing cards while they watched over a pregnant girl. He didn't like the inaction. He couldn't stand her odd craving and when she had to pee, he found it uncomfortable to stand by the door while she relieved herself. And she peed *a lot*. The only redeeming quality was that she was nice to look at. "Pinky," he whispered. "When do you think we'll be done babysitting? I'm getting bored."

Pinky nodded. "Me too. I wish the old man would come back."

They both turned an eye towards Veronica who was washing her bowl and spoon in the sink before placing them both in the drainer.

"Gentlemen?" boomed the voice from the second-floor office. "Your presence is requested."

Grizz and Pinky stopped playing cards and ran over to the stairs, looking upward. "Ask and you'll receive," Pinky said out of the corner of his mouth. Veronica turned toward the voice, wiping her hands on a small dish towel that hung in front of the sink.

"Up here, you..." The old man paused. "Please come up the stairs for this discussion."

The two thugs did as they were told. Once at the top of the stairs, they crept towards the window. The old man behind the glass lowered his voice so Veronica couldn't hear. "It seems we have a problem. And I need you to take care of it pronto."

Grizz looked at Pinky with a grin. Maybe the boredom was about to be replaced? They both needed a little action and the boss was giving them their chance.

"What would you like us to do," Pinky asked.

A manilla envelope slid under the door. Pinky picked it up and opened it, pulling out two pictures.

"Everything you need is in the envelope," the old man instructed. "These two have been investigating our little operation and frankly, they recently got a little too close for comfort. I want you to communicate to them to back off on their efforts. The last thing we need is a couple of wanna-be detectives to interfere with our plan. Have I made myself clear?"

"Yes sir," said Pinky. He handed the envelope to his partner who also looked at the photos.

"Now," commanded the voice. "When you've accomplished your task, I'll come back for your report. And don't forget the girl."

Grizz answered, momentarily forgetting his place in the hierarchy. "How could we forg…" Pinky jammed an elbow into the big man's ribs, causing Grizz to stop.

This time it was his turn to talk out of the side of his mouth, complaining, "Ouch."

When there was no response from the old man, the two thugs relaxed knowing he'd left. Walking down the steps, they were met by Veronica, her hands planted on her hips.

"Well," she said. "What's up?"

Pinky waved a finger at her. "None of your concern. We gotta go take care of some business. And you know what that means." He made a head bob towards the chair, indicating she would have to once again be restrained.

"Aww fellas," she complained. "You don't have to do that. I'm not going anywhere. Puh-leeze!"

Her cries were ignored as Pinky escorted her to the chair. "You gotta pee first?" he asked.

Veronica shook her head and sat down. Pinky secured her and then placed a fresh piece of duct tape across her mouth.

"We'll be back shortly," he said, re-checking his knots.

"Yea, shortly," mimicked Grizz. As Pinky joined him, they walked together towards their car for the task at hand. Grizz took one more look at the two pictures. "Not bored anymore," he said as he shoved the photos of the two problems, Axel and Kennedy, into the envelope.

# Chapter Twelve

As Kennedy drove back to Veronica's house, Axel recounted his close call. "I missed her by this much," Axel explained, holding his right hand up in pinch mode. "This much."

"You said it was a woman, did you get a good look at her?" Kennedy pressed. "Could you give a description?"

"I could have reached out and touched the woman. But it happened so fast, I didn't pay attention. I open doors for lots of people. It's the boy scout in me. All I know is she had brown hair, but she looked like a normal middle-aged woman. Did you see her?"

"No," said the ex-butler. "And if I did, she didn't register. I was focusing on the PO box, not the postal workers. And if she was in there, I didn't see her approach the box."

Axel thought for a moment. "Unless she got there before we did. The postal worker said she had just canceled the box number. But why did she do that?"

Kennedy shrugged. "Perhaps when the old man went into the FALM and her checks stopped she may have not seen the need. Without checks, why pay for a postal box?"

"And that was our only connection to the brown-haired woman," Axel complained.

Kennedy nodded. "I'm afraid so. Unless you can find out who Benton was sending money to."

Axel contemplated this thought. "Going back through the bank records, the only thing I can think of were the checks he was sending out marked 'Cash.' They had no name listed."

"Well, that's a start. Just go to the bank and check the name on the back of the check who endorsed them." Catching Axel's eyebrow-raising look, Kennedy corrected his error. "Oh sorry. You no longer oversee the estate so no more access to bank records. Damn."

Both men contemplated the lost opportunity. The woman, much like the contents of PO Box 212, was gone.

"So now what?" asked Axel. "Where do we go from here?"

"Inside," he said as he parked the car in Veronica's drive. "I'll make some coffee."

They entered the house and Kennedy went straight to the kitchen to put on a pot. He came back out and headed for the piano hiding spot, producing the pages from the ledger. Placing them on the table he began to scan. "Maybe we can find another clue," he said, as if gazing into the pages would magically answer all their questions. But the documents remained silent.

"If these pages could talk," Kennedy said as he aimlessly poured over them. "There are a lot of people who Benton had control over. Not to mention, any illegal activities resulting from that control."

"Yeah, it is amazing where the old octopus had his tentacles, isn't it?" Axel pondered. "Now that he's back, I wonder what evil plans he has for this town of ours."

"Hmmm," Kennedy murmured, looking at one entry.

"You found something?" Axel asked hopefully.

"No, this one entry reminded me of a good deed I did. Glad something good came out of this damn thing," he said. "We're at a dead end. Time to get back on the path to finding Veronica." With that declaration, Kennedy gathered up the pages and placed them back in the bowels of the piano.

"Any suggestions?" Axel asked. But before Kennedy could answer, the doorbell rang and the two men looked at each other in puzzlement as neither was expecting visitors. Kennedy went to the door and opened it.

It was a smiling Bulldog.

"Good afternoon, Mr. Kennedy," the assistant chief said. "Let's go for a ride, shall we?"

"We're kind of busy at the moment, sir," responded Kennedy, standing up straight and pulling on the base of his coat. "Could we reschedule for another time?" He smiled in an attempt to subdue the fear.

"Nope," replied the Bulldog. "This time we're doing it my way. Turn around, you're under arrest."

Axel stood by dumbfounded as the Bulldog read Kennedy his Miranda rights before pushing him into the back seat of the patrol car, careful not to bump the ex-butler's head on the door frame.

As they drove towards the police station, Kennedy asked, "Officer, Why on earth would you arrest me? I've done nothing wrong; you have no proof I've committed a crime. We spoke of this forgery business before, so what has changed?"

The Bulldog never turned around, keeping his eyes on the road. "I arrested you because I know you're guilty. And I'm never wrong. I also suspect someone else is also part of this deception. Forgery could get either one of you time in prison. How would you like an extended stay at the Hotel Incarceration?"

When Kennedy didn't respond, the Bulldog continued, "The way I see it, you have two options: One, you plead guilty, and my job is done."

"And the second option?" asked the unflappable Kennedy.

"Here's the fun part. If you don't plead guilty, I'll go after someone else."

"And who may that be?" Kennedy asked, his unflappable demeanor wavering, already aware of the answer.

"If you don't fess up. I'm going after Ahearne. And when I get my teeth into him, trust me, I won't let go. And the one thing that changed?" The Bulldog responded; a grin plastered across his face. "Harley Benton is pressing charges. Ruff, Ruff."

Kennedy sat back in his seat, taking the Miranda advice deciding it best to remain silent. Given the choice, he came to the stark conclusion if anyone was going to get caught in the jaws of the Bulldog, it wouldn't be Axel.

Axel watched anxiously as Kennedy was ushered into the jail's cafeteria where friends, relatives, and lawyers came to visit with the incarcerated.

Kennedy smirked softly and lifted his hands, showing handcuffs. "How do you like my new jewelry?" he asked Axel. The officer unlocked the cuffs and withdrew with them in hand.

"How can you laugh at a time like this?" Axel asked, aghast at the treatment of his good friend. Kennedy may have had some errors of judgment in his youth, but nothing that required handcuffs.

"In a situation like this, why wouldn't one choose to joke? I assure you, sir, the alternative is not pretty."

Axel leaned in as if no one in the crowded room could hear their conversation. "Do the police have any evidence?" he asked.

"Not sure. Most of it would be circumstantial. The only one who could verify a forgery…" Now it was Kennedy's turn to lean in. "Wasn't even in the room. Am I correct?"

"If you say so."

Kennedy stretched before leaning back in. "Now that Benton has regained control, he is using leverage by pressing charges to get his revenge. He didn't take kindly to me siding with you. That is why it is of the utmost importance for you to stay out of this fight. He's still dangerous. But it is evidence, not leverage, which leads to convictions. And he doesn't have any solid evidence."

"I understand. Now what? Have they set a court date? Bond?"

"Not until I speak with my attorney. And I do not want you putting up bail money. Is that understood? They might let me out because I have no priors. Helping the police thwart corruption earlier this year cannot hurt my case."

Nervously, Axel fidgeted. "What can I do, then?"

"I'm glad you asked. I need a few favors. Can you handle them for me?"

"Sure. You know I'd do anything for you. What do you need?"

Kennedy began, "One, call Harold Grange. I want him to represent me."

Axel nodded. He saw the benefit in this. Harold Grange, the ex-Benton attorney knew them both. He also had a good reason to take the case. Karma.

"And I need another favor, I'm going to forego a jury trial and leave it up to the judge. I need you to mail a stack of letters today. They're on the kitchen table. And don't ask why," he cautioned. Seeing that Axel was confused, he ended their meeting with a thought.

"Axel, I've had bad luck before. And I'm not a good gambler. But this time instead of letting luck play my hand, I think it is time to hedge my bet. And after this, you are out of the Harley Benton business for good, do you understand?"

Nodding, Axel left his friend with the two requests in mind, hoping Kennedy knew what he was doing.

About a mile into his drive home and his mind occupied with his incarcerated friend's wellbeing, Axel failed to see the black sedan come screaming up behind him, but he heard it before it could slam into his rear bumper. Snapping out of his self-imposed thoughts, Axel instinctively pushed on the accelerator, his head pressing back into the headrest. Axel was not a reckless driver. Anything but. However, his fight-or-flight reflex had kicked in.

Axel was also not a fighter. His one advantage was that he'd grown up in this town and he knew the roads. The black sedan stayed on his tail and Axel braced himself for a collision of bumpers. It never came, as he took a sharp right turn down Bush Hill Road. This was a road with few homes scattered sporadically, perfect for teenagers to make out or party with plenty of privacy. He vaguely remembered what Leif and his friends used to call it while in high school. "Bullshit Road."

In his rearview mirror, he saw the front grill of the sedan racing towards him. Panicking, he tried to plan his next move. The sedan was creeping toward him and out in this remote part of town, whatever the driver wanted to do with him once stopped, would have no eyes or ears to serve as witnesses.

He took a left turn, spitting up dirt from the side of the road. The sedan turned left as well and was gaining again. Axel knew there was a T in the road coming up. He had three choices; left, right, or straight into the tree by the ditch. Here goes, he thought. *Hope this works.*

Turning on his right turn signal, he began to turn right. Almost immediately, he reversed course, his tires screaming as they kicked up a cloud of dust. The tail of his car slid precariously close to the ditch almost hitting the trunk of the tree with his rear fender, but Axel corrected and sped off to his left. Looking into the rearview mirror he waited. He thought he might have ditched his pursuers when through the cloud of dust came the black sedan.

"Shit!" he yelled, panic now gripping him in its firm clutch. "What do you want!" he yelled. A thought arose frightening him further. Axel's parents had died in an auto accident. What if he died in one as well? Axel had nearly lost his life in one earlier this year, what if this time he was not so lucky? And how would Winnie cope with another loss? He shook the thoughts from his head, replacing them with a line from his dead brother, completely missing the irony.

*We're all going to die, but not me and not today.*

Emboldened by his brother's words, Axel knew what to do next. He waited until the sedan caught up. He knew if he let the car behind him run into his back bumper, it would slow his pursuer down, forcing the driver to hit the gas once again. Axel laid off the accelerator and braced for the collision. The sedan smashed into Axel's bumper, jostling him around in the driver's seat. But it had the desired effect as Axel floored the car once again, this time turning hard left and watching as the black sedan sped up and drove past the turn. He knew it would turn and chase him but that's exactly what Axel wanted. He might not be able to fight the pursuer, but he sure as hell could outsmart him.

Axel drove on a quarter of a mile waiting for the sedan to come into view. When it did, he nodded in approval. He floored it once again and took a series of right and left turns, keeping the sedan on his tail, but not allowing the vehicle the ability to approach and get closer than a few car lengths.

The last turn Axel made, put him on Lexington Street. It was more congested than the back roads with apartment buildings, storefronts, and restaurants on either side. There was also another building at the end of the street. Axel knew what it was. He was hoping the sedan's driver didn't.

Axel slowed down as the sedan caught up and as soon as the pursuer was within a car length and closing, Axel slammed on his brakes and pulled into a parking lot. The sedan swerved to avoid his rear bumper, then slowed as they passed the one building they wanted no part of. The Benton Falls Police Department.

Axel, sweating and tired, took a deep breath. Proud of himself for his craftiness. He was glad to realize he was right. Knowing a town is so much safer than not.

His cell phone vibrated, startling him. It was Winnie. Begrudgingly he took the call.

"Hello, Winnie," answered Axel.

"Where are you, son," Winnie asked. "Have you been jogging? You sound as if you just finished a marathon."

"No, I'm fine." *Not me and not today.*

"I wanted to know if you had found anything else out about Veronica."

"Winnie," said Axel, his frustration coming out. "I told you to let us handle this! How many times do I have to tell you, this isn't a job for an old woman? Now please stay out of our way."

"But I have some news…" Winnie began before Axel rudely cut her off.

"Look, I have too many things on my plate and I don't have time for this nonsense. I'm at the police station. Kennedy's been arrested and I just got chased by a pretty angry driver in a black sedan and I don't know why. It's not like I flipped him the bird or cut him off. So, if you don't mind, please stop calling me for updates, OK?"

"Wait, Kennedy's in jail? And a black sedan you say? Jules and I have been trackin'…" Axel once again cut his grandmother off.

"Winnie, for the love of Pete. Look, I'll call you later and fill you in. Right now, I need to report this crazy driver."

As he hung up, he shook his head, wondering how he could stop his grandmother from interfering. He got out of the car and was about to head up the stairs of the station when the black sedan slowly drove past. There was a small man in the passenger seat gesturing to Axel with an index finger that moved back and forth like the pendulum of a metronome.

"What the hell?" Axel asked aloud, unsure what he'd done to these two menaces. He was, however, very sure what the gesture meant. And it wasn't good.

"First of all," began the old man from his perch on the second floor. "You kidnapped the wrong woman. Secondly, you put the ransom note where only *she* could find it. Thirdly, you brazenly go into the nursing home to abduct the Ahearne woman…in broad daylight and in front of witnesses, no less. And to top it off, you can't even scare a guy into stopping his investigation of us. This whole operation has been a cluster… Whatever do you have to say for yourselves?"

Pinky and Grizz stood silently at the base of the staircase. Both shuffled their feet, awaiting the other to take the lead. Neither volunteered.

"WELL? I'm waiting." The old man seemed really pissed now. Pinky stepped forward, *It's better to take the lead. Let the big guy look weak.*

"I understand that I…" rectifying his mistake, he pointed at Grizz. "WE have made some errors, sir, But I think we did scare the Ahearne fella pretty bad. I don't think he'll be sticking his nose into our business again."

Grizz found his courage, chiming in, "Yeah, if he didn't stop at the police station, we'd have caught him and taught him a lesson he wouldn't forget."

"Boys," came the voice. "Whatever am I going to do with you?"

Emboldened, Pinky replied, "Let us finish the job. We have an appointment with the old woman later this afternoon. We'll nab her and be out of there before anyone knows she's gone. Then, we'll drop her off here, get paid, and disappear where no one will be able to find us."

The old man seemed to be placated by the confidence shown by Pinky. He softened his tone. "All right. Mr. Kennedy is in jail, so we can't touch him. You better be right about the

Ahearne boy. Now it's time to finish the job. And no more mistakes. Today is the only window of opportunity so you better get in then out quickly."

Pinky was relieved the old man took his suggestion. But something nagged at him. Instead of getting yelled at, or worse, the old man allowed them to continue the mission. Wiping a bead of sweat from his forehead, he heard a door close from above. Taking a chance, he called up the stairs. No answer. The old man had once again left them. A sense of dread settled into his stomach. *That was way too easy.*

"Sorry you guys got in trouble," Veronica said, from the sink. "I know these people. They are pretty crafty."

Both men gave her a dirty look, causing her to turn back to washing the dishes. Silently.

Pinky pondered the last exchange. They *had* made a lot of mistakes. In New York and now here. In their business, you shouldn't make too many. The consequences proved fatal. *Something ain't right.*

He sat down at the table watching Grizz shuffle the deck. *Wonder if he senses it too?*

"Boy, we got out of that one, eh?" The big man said, loudly blowing out a breath of relief.

"Yeah," said Pinky, surmising Grizz had no idea what trouble the two could be in for. "We got outta that one," he answered, but his gut told him otherwise.

Will entered Harley Benton's room as the old man sat upright in bed, his right hand making a fist, then releasing while his left hand followed suit.

"Good. It looks like you're improving," he told the old man. "How's the speech?"

"Bettah," explained the old man.

"Look," Will said, an uncomfortable expression crossing his face. "You've asked me to help you and I think I've done an adequate job. Now it's time you helped me. I don't like all the mystery surrounding us. I need you to tell me what's going on."

"I can help with that," came an answer from behind him. In his haste to speak with the old man, he failed to notice Arabella standing against the far wall.

"Mom?" he said, the shock apparent. "What are you doing here?"

Arabella placed her hands on her hips and cocked her head. "Will, he sent for me. You gave me the note. So now I'm here." She gave a quizzical look at Benton. "You want to tell him? Or should I?"

"Tell me what?" Will stood frozen.

Benton waved his good hand at Arabella. "You," he said clearly. "Go ahet."

"Well dear son, it seems we have a little secret we've been keeping from you," Arabella said. "It's time for the truth." She took a few steps and sidled up to Will, pulling a chair up to the back of his legs. "I think you may want to sit for this. There's no sense in having two of you bedridden." When Will remained standing, she pushed him gently into the chair.

"Remember what I told you happened to your father?" she asked. It wasn't said in malice or regret, just factual. Will nodded. Then to Benton, she explained. "I told him his dad was killed fighting in the Middle East."

"Are you telling me he didn't?" Will tried to stand, but his mother laid a gentle hand against his shoulder.

"Yes. He didn't. And I would have held off telling you the truth today if it wasn't absolutely necessary. Certain circumstances have presented themselves so the truth will…no, *needs* to come out. Because you, my son, are part of the plan."

Will shook his head to clear it. It didn't work. Looking at Benton he asked, "Do you know the truth?" Benton eyed the young man and nodded slowly. Looking back at his mother, he took a deep breath before asking the question. "So, what is the truth? Is Mr. Benton my grandfather?"

Benton's eyebrows raised unevenly. Arabella took a step back, put a hand to her lips, and stifled a laugh. "No, no. He's not your grandfather." Smiling, she added, "But it was an interesting guess."

"I'm sorry about that, Mr. Benton. I've been wracking my brain to figure out all the secrecy and it just seemed logical." Turning back to his mother he asked, "And what plan that I'm a part of are you talking about?"

Benton reached out his right hand and patted the boy's arm as if to ask for his patience.

"Hold on, son," Arabella cautioned. "No, he's not your grandfather." She gave Benton a knowing look Will found odd until he heard her last sentence.

"He's your *father.*"

# Chapter Thirteen

"All rise," said the bailiff, stiffening his spine as if these would be the most important words he would utter all day. Kennedy and his lawyer did as instructed and rose to face arraignment.

Axel sat behind Kennedy and as the ex-butler rose, Axel touched his sleeve in encouragement. This caused Kennedy to turn toward the young man with a reassuring nod and smile.

Looking past Axel, Kennedy noticed the Bulldog sitting a few rows behind him, a malevolent expression aimed his way. His smile faded slowly, giving away his resignation to the notion this was a serious matter with retribution forthcoming. He deserved it, especially feeling guilty about the ancient hit-and-run crime committed against Axel's parents.

He also felt guilty he'd put Axel into positions that threatened his freedom. If Karma was a bitch, his had an awful temper. Adding to his discomfort was the fact Winnie and Jules were not in attendance. He understood their job of finding Veronica took precedence, but their absence was still distressing.

Again, his feeling of remorse was overshadowed by his need for penance. And forgiveness.

As for the Bulldog, Kennedy's concern for Axel's safety was secure. He'd found a way to save his friend. As far as he was concerned, the assistant chief could go to hell.

Judge Amos Cyrus Colson sat down and waved the courtroom to do the same. According to Kennedy's lawyer, Judge Colson heeded a strict code of decorum in his courtroom. He gave some latitude but tolerated no theatrics. State your case, let the facts decide innocence or guilt, then let's go home.

The judge cleared his throat as he reviewed the docket. "The State versus Brogan Kennedy. Sir, you've been charged with forgery. The alteration of a legal document with intent to defraud. Do you understand the charges?"

"I understand," Kennedy answered, his chin held high as he watched the judge shuffle his court pages.

Kennedy had hired Harold Grange to represent him for good reason, valuing the work the attorney had completed for the Benton Foundation and felt he was a capable lawyer. It also occurred to Kennedy the man might have an axe to grind against the one who recently had him fired. Kennedy would not need to provide the axe or grinding wheel today.

Grange gave his client a reassuring look. The plan was to enter a plea of not guilty so they would have a chance to go to trial and win. There was no solid proof Kennedy had committed the fraud by signing Benton's will. "We can walk out of here today," the lawyer had promised.

Benton's attorney, Carlton Flack, stood and addressed the judge, "Your Honor, before we begin, two requests from my client. One, we made an earlier petition to recuse Attorney

Harold Grange from representing his client in this case. Have you made a decision?"

Judge Colson eyed Benton's lawyer. "On conflict of interest?"

Flack puffed out his chest. "Yes, Your Honor. He was my client, Mr. Harley Benton's lawyer until just recently."

"Didn't your client *fire* Counselor Grange?"

Flack let out a breath. "Yes sir, he did."

"Then, no. Petition denied. This isn't a non-compete issue. You can't have it both ways. Mr. Grange has a right to make a living also."

Kennedy noticed the look of surprise on Benton's face. Kennedy wasn't surprised at all.

The judge continued, "Any more requests?"

Deflated, Flack tried to puff his chest out once more but failed. "There are some missing documents from my client's office and we believe the defense is in possession of these documents. My client would like them returned."

The judge looked over his glasses toward Carlton Flack. "What kind of documents?"

Pleased, Kennedy knew exactly what Benton was looking for. And he felt confident the judge did as well. The ex-butler surmised Flack had found Benton's hiding spot empty, reveling in the fact that he kept a copy of the ledger in a hiding spot of his own.

"They are of a *sensitive* nature," Flack answered. "Having to do with certain *financial* arrangements."

In Kennedy's assessment, this last statement felt as if directed at the judge. They are sensitive, alright, thought Kennedy. *If the public only knew.*

The judge was unflappable. "Could you be more specific, Mr. Flack? How will we know what to retrieve if we don't know what they are?"

Benton pulled on Flack's sleeve with his good hand before using it to spin a notepad in front of the lawyer. Flack read the note, looked up at the judge, and asked, "Permission to approach?"

The judge flicked two fingers, summoning both lawyers to his bench.

Flack began. "The information we're looking for is of a very serious nature, Your Honor. If it becomes public it will harm my client." He then leaned in and whispered to the judge, "As well as other members of the community."

The judge looked amused. Kennedy noticed this sentiment seemed to confuse Flack as if the attorney was expecting a different reaction.

"Harm?" the judge asked. "In what way?"

Flack rubbed his forehead. "In a financial way with potential repercussions to my client's reputation. You see, the documents in question are a record of, er…loans." He stopped as if to gauge the judge's reaction. He didn't get one so he continued to press. "Monies that people have borrowed from my very generous client over the years." Still no reaction from the judge. "If he doesn't retrieve the led... the documents, it will cost him a financial hardship, which in turn could damage his reputation." Flack once again stopped. The judge wore a blank expression, so the lawyer tried once more to plead his case. "And the reputation of *others* if it were to ever be made public…."

On hearing Flack's last statement, Kennedy noticed the judge shift uncomfortably in his chair. He also knew why.

Flack's attempts at veiled threats to expose the judge were subtle to the courtroom but not to Kennedy or the judge.

Judge Colson looked past the lawyers at Mr. Kennedy, who gave a small, yet imperceptible shake of his head.

Recovering his composure, the judge turned to Grange. "You were his lawyer for many years. Do you have any idea what documents Mr. Flack is referring to?"

Kennedy found this game of cat and mouse amusing. He also knew it would present a hardship to more than Harley Benton should the documents become public.

Counselor Grange put his hands on the judge's desk and responded. "I do not, Your Honor. Perhaps it might help if Mr. Flack describes what he's looking for?"

"Good idea." Turning to Flack, Judge Colson asked "Counselor, what form do these 'documents' take?"

Flack looked bewildered. "I'm not sure what you mean, your honor."

"Then let me help you. Are these financial documents on paper? In a notebook? A computer spreadsheet?"

Flack turned to look at Benton who wore a scowl. "May I confer with my client?"

"Oh, by all means, be my guest." The judge delivered a sweeping hand motion. "We'll wait." Light laughter filled the courtroom as Flack spoke with his client. He came back to the bench but did not look happy. "Your Honor," Flack began. "My client does not want to describe the documents due to their sensitive nature. Surely, your honor, you can understand certain financial records should remain confidential, don't you?"

This time, Flack's question to sway the judge was not so subtle. It was also destined to fail.

"Well, there's your answer, Your Honor," lawyer Grange said. "If he can't describe it, we can't find it to enter into evidence."

Flack waved his hands back and forth, "No, no, my client doesn't want it into evidence. He just wants it returned to him."

Grange jumped in, "Then why are we discussing…"

Judge Colson put up one hand to silence both lawyers. "Once you can describe the documents you want us to find and their *relevance* to this case, we'll revisit the issue. In the meantime, we have a trial to finish. Let's get back to it, shall we?"

Grange looked pleased at winning the point. The judge looked relieved. Flack looked sullen. Kennedy held a small grin as he looked over at the still scowling Harley Benton.

Benton wanted his ledger back. Kennedy knew any business profits didn't come close to the value the leverage of the ledger provided. He would make sure Benton would never again see the papers from the copied ledger he possessed. And he was confident Kepner wouldn't hand over the part Kennedy had passed on to him. It was labeled 'Evidence' and stored securely at police headquarters. Mr. Kennedy had effectively castrated the old geezer's power by retiring the debt and destroying the original evidence. *It would be fun to watch the old man's reaction, once he's found out what I've done.*

With that said, it was time to end this one chapter in his life and begin the next. Kennedy had been running from the guilt of both his past and the crimes committed. He no longer felt the need to run. He also heeded the Bulldog's threat to go after Master Axel. He couldn't let that happen. There would be no more running or walking. Penance, forgiveness, and peace of mind would only come from remorse and justice. It was time to stand still.

Judge Colson was ready to move on. He asked Kennedy to rise. "How do you plead?"

Lawyer Grange stood up to speak, but Kennedy put a hand on the man's arm, indicating he'd enter the plea himself.

"Guilty, Your Honor," Kennedy announced to a shocked courtroom. "Guilty."

Hector walked down the hall whistling a happy tune, his left hand in his pocket rubbing the Tag-It! between his thumb and forefinger like an Irish worry stone. Yet there was no worry for him this afternoon. He loved his new job, was making more money than he'd dreamed, had the respect of the residents and employees alike, and best of all, his workload had been lessened considerably by adding Will Ames to the team. The young man was doing a tremendous job.

When he got back to his office, he'd begin the search for another orderly. Even if Hector could find another person with half the qualities of his new charge, he would be a happier man indeed. If he knew what awaited him on his desk, his happiness would evaporate like rain on a sun-scorched sidewalk.

Unaware of the impending unwelcome news, Hector happily patrolled the halls of the FALM, where he spotted Winnie and gave her a wide salute. Winnie stopped him.

"Just the man I wanted to see. Give me your keys please." Hector stopped rubbing the small disc and pulled out his keys, handing them to his boss before asking, "Are you going to the trial?"

Winnie sighed and gazed heavenward. "Ah, blessed are those who get prosecuted like the prophets before them," she said. Then straightening her posture, she added. "No, those boys can take care of themselves. I have bigger things to worry on." Winnie pulled the Tag-It! from the chain. "You have this synced to your phone?" she asked.

"Yes, ma'am," he responded.

"Good," she said as she put it in her pocket. "I'll return it later. Meanwhile, keep your phone handy in case I need you." She tossed him the keys and he slipped them into his right hand pocket.

Disappointed his new tool was gone, he responded, "Sure, bos… I mean Miss Winnie. Anything you need." She left him standing there as she picked up a brisk pace.

"Miss Winnie?" he called after her, wanting to offer his services for whatever she was up to. She didn't turn around, instead, put a hand to her ear representing a phone. "In case I need you," she yelled over her shoulder.

He now felt he did need an actual worry stone. Negative thoughts crept into his head and he couldn't dislodge them. Wondering what she wanted with his Tag-It! he opened the app on his phone and watched intently as the green dot representing his boss showed her leaving the building, then leaving the premises too quickly to be on foot. He wished she'd asked him to drive her wherever she wanted to go. As the chief of security, you'd think he would be called upon to protect her. This thought deepened his worry and disappointment.

He scrolled the app off and placed his phone into his left pant pocket. Sliding a hand into his right pocket to find his keys without the Tag-It! Hector slouched as he continued his afternoon rounds, wondering two things. Would he get his joyful feeling back today? And where was Miss Winnie headed with his Tag-It? He doubted the first and for the second, prayed it was someplace safe.

It was fifteen minutes before two o'clock when Winnie instructed Jules to find a spot at the end of the parking lot across from the construction site. She did as the old woman asked but questioned her, "Wait, we were just here yesterday. What gives?"

"You said something that got under my skin. 'Hiding in plain sight.' I have a hunch. This is a site and it's plain to see I need to do a little investigative work. We don't have much time."

Winnie looked at her phone before turning it towards Jules. "That's the black sedan," she mentioned casually, pointing to the green dot while looking for a reaction from Jules. She didn't get one so either Jules was a really cool customer or Axel failed to tell her about being chased by the black sedan. If Axel protected his girlfriend from a scare like that, Winnie felt she could as well. Jules would find out soon enough.

The women watched the black sedan of the two 'visitors' leave the construction site from the back, headed toward the FALM right on schedule. Winnie prayed Dottie could stall them sufficiently so she could either check this location off the list or find their girl.

"Keep the car running," ordered Winnie.

The five-story building's bottom floor was framed and boarded up in some places with plywood, in others, sheets of plastic to ward against inclement weather as rain pelted the structure. Crews were busy with electrical and HVAC work, hammers clanged and saws buzzed noisily as Winnie left the car, putting on the hood from her jacket, concerned more about her health than appearance.

This structure, a skeleton of I-beams awaiting their turn for completion would soon house retail space, a restaurant or two, dry cleaner, or coffee shop. Above, four floors of living space were planned. Getting closer, Winnie could see there was no place to hide here. She wasn't so sure there wasn't another place or why would the black sedan lead her here? Her intuition and curious nature took over. She stepped off the sidewalk and into the buzz of construction, sidestepping lumber, tools, and wiring. Watching the guys go about their business once again prompted the image of those TV show construction puppets. *Doozers.*

There was a hard hat lying on a pile of wallboard so she picked it up and tried to put it on to blend in, keeping her eyes open for any place suitable for storing a pregnant girl.

Fumbling the helmet, it clattered on the floor. Quickly picking it up, she looked around to see if anyone had noticed. The helmet noise was subdued by the ongoing construction fracas and each worker seemed too busy with their own work, so she put the helmet on securely and began walking.

Trying to avoid a step ladder, she brushed her shoulder against one leg. "Oh shit!" she heard from above, followed by a dull thud on the cement, as a screw gun landed near her feet, missing her head by mere inches.

"Watch it, will ya!" screamed the man on the ladder. Seeing who he was yelling at, he calmed his tone somewhat. "A little help?" he asked. Winnie picked up the tool and tossed it back to the man. He tipped the brim of his hard hat in thanks and went back to work. Winnie pressed on, her head on a swivel hoping not to make any more mistakes.

Making her way to the back of the site, she found a sheet of plastic hanging over an open space that served as an exit. She grabbed the edge and was about to open it when she felt a hand on her shoulder.

"Hey, can I help you with something?" a large man shouted over the din. He was dressed as a typical Doozer; hard hat, tool belt, jeans, and a short-sleeved shirt that barely covered his beer belly.

"What?" Winnie yelled back. She had been startled and needed a moment to recover. She heard what the man had said but was stalling while she thought.

"I said, can I help you?"

Collecting herself, Winnie yelled back, "Yeah, you can! I'm from City Ordinance. Where's your construction permit?"

As a former restaurant owner, Winnie learned two things. One, The city loved to have surprise inspections, and two, whenever she was confronted by anyone, either a government official or an unruly patron, confidence always trumped fear.

The Doozer looked confused. "Where did you say you were from?"

Winnie showed impatience. "The city, dammit! THE CITY! Look I haven't got all day!"

Her phone rang and she stuck up a finger. "Hold on," she yelled at the Doozer.

"Miss Winnie, it's Dottie. Your appointment is here. They seem anxious so I don't know how long I can keep them."

"Hey, no worries. Stick to the plan. Thanks." Winnie hit the hang-up button but continued to talk looking up at the large man in front of her, "Yea, I'm here now. I'm talkin' with…" holding the phone to her chest, she asked, "What's your name?"

"Doug. Doug Clawson."

Putting the phone to her ear she repeated loudly. "A Doug Clawson. Yeah, I know, I know. I'm trying to get it now!" She put the phone back against her chest. Time was running out before those thugs would return. "You want my boss to come down here to talk with your boss?"

The Doozer shook his head. Winnie brought the free hand up, cupping her mouth, and yelled, "Then get me the damn permit!"

Weighing his options, Doug scratched his chin. Winnie could tell he didn't want both the city and his boss on-site at the same time. "I'll be right back with it," he said and hurried away to find the document.

As soon as he was out of sight, Winnie slipped past the plastic sheet and stood on the concrete slab to stay out of the rain and the mud. Behind the building sat more construction material, a few pieces of equipment… and a two-story cement structure. A metal door stood at each end of the building and a rack of windows ran across the top just under the flat roof. This can't be it, she thought. There's too much going on. *The Doozers would have to be morons not to notice a pregnant kidnap victim.*

Shaking her head, Winnie turned to leave when she remembered something Jules stated: A perfect place to hold a kidnapping was the right site *in plain sight*. Turning back toward the concrete building, she inspected it once more, just to make sure. She gazed up at the windows and noticed half were clean. The other half filthy. "That's odd," she whispered. She followed the panes to the far corner window. It was clean like the others yet there was a white object attached to the bottom left-hand corner. Winnie squinted trying to identify it. That didn't work, so she took out her cell phone and opened her camera app for a better look. The object was still fuzzy, so she walked along the side of the building, careful not to step into the mud. Pinching the screen as Hector had taught allowed her to magnify the object. This made her look twice; the first time in disbelief, the second in recognition.

A smile came across her face as she pushed the hard hat up over her forehead scratching just above her left eyebrow. *Clever girl.*

Stuck in the window was a sheet of paper with a drawing. A bald-headed angel, its halo tipped fashionably to one side.

# Chapter Fourteen

An audible gasp arose from the courtroom as Kennedy repeated his plea. "Guilty, Your Honor."

"Are you sure?" asked Judge Colson.

Without hesitation, Kennedy answered. "I am Your Honor."

Harold Grange looked down at the table, shaking his head in disbelief. With Kennedy's guilty plea, his job seemed done for the day.

The judge skewered his mouth in contemplation as to what to say next. "Before sentencing, tell me," he asked. "What prompted you to do so? Forgery is a serious crime."

Kennedy stood straight, as only an ex-butler could. Then, before speaking, he looked over at Harley Benton. The old man had replaced the scowl with a sneer.

"Your Honor, at the time, Mr. Benton had just experienced a major stroke. I had worked for him for several years and saw the damage he had done to this fine town and its residents and felt I could, in this way, help to lessen that damage." He paused to let the next statement carry more weight. "I also felt the need to ease my conscience for my years of complicit silence."

He stared straight forward, not wanting to again look at Harley Benton, but others in the courtroom did. Axel would later inform him how everyone else turned toward the old man, adding, "If looks could kill, there'd be no need for a trial."

Carlton Flack, jumped up. "Your Honor, my client, Mr. Benton is not on trial here. Mr. Kennedy has admitted his crime. It should be an open and shut case."

During this exchange, Axel leaned forward and handed Grange an envelope. The lawyer read it quickly and turned back to Axel, who winked at the counselor. Grange nodded in recognition then turned toward the judge.

"Your Honor. It is correct that my client is pleading guilty. However, If I may have a little latitude."

The judge nodded his approval.

"The law defines forgery as the act of falsifying information for *personal gain*," Grange said as he picked up the folder and waved it in the air. "These are tax records and checks made out to Mr. Kennedy. I'd like to submit them into evidence."

Benton looked at his own lawyer who stood to object. "Your Honor, the man admitted to forgery and his own lawyer is showing documents Mr. Kennedy, as a paid employee, did indeed profit from his crime. Therefore, we should consider larceny charges in addition to forgery."

The judge looked over at the defense table. "Well?"

"This is where it gets very clear, Your Honor. According to the records I have in my possession, Mr. Kennedy was never compensated by the Benton estate. He was compensated by the estate of Mr. Leif Ahearne, the deceased brother of Mr. Axel Ahearne the former overseer of the Benton Estate."

Harold Grange brought the documents to the judge, followed closely by Flack, sputtering about "discovery," and the lack thereof.

"This just came into our possession this morning, Your Honor," the lawyer said, holding back the grin that threatened to bubble up.

Surprised, Kennedy turned to Axel. The young man had no qualms about showing his pleasure. It seemed the former accountant not only knew how to lie but also to use the law to protect his friend from jeopardy.

Flack protested, "Mr. Kennedy lives on the Benton estate. Doesn't that count as 'compensation?'"

Grange shot a glance to Axel who pointed at the file as if to say, "It's in there."

"Counselor?" the judge questioned, as Grange shuffled through the paperwork.

"Here it is Your Honor. I have records here that prove Mr. Kennedy does indeed live on the Benton Estate. He uses his old bedroom."

Flack interrupted, "Well, there you have it, Your Honor. Compensation."

Grange put a finger in the air to continue, "Your Honor, I'm not finished. Mr. Kennedy is not compensated for the use of the estate. In fact, it's just the opposite because Mr. Kennedy pays the Benton estate rent!" He offered the intel to the judge first, who nodded, then to Flack, who frowned.

Both lawyers went back to their tables as Grange once again asked the judge for the floor.

"Any objections, counselor?" the judge asked Benton's lawyer. Benton's scowl deepened.

"No, Your Honor," Flack answered, his sarcastic tone coming through. "Even *I'd* like to hear what my esteemed colleague has to say next." This remark elicited laughter from the crowd but a stern look from the judge quieted the courtroom.

"Your Honor," began Grange. "Mr. Kennedy didn't have to plead guilty. In fact, he could have gone to trial and chances are he could have been found *not* guilty. He did so because he is an honorable man. He knows he did wrong but did not do so for his own profit."

The lawyer came from around the table, waving his arm out towards the crowded courtroom. "He forged the signature for the people of this town. So their lives would be better. Here are some facts to support my argument: In the last six months of Mr. Ahearne's stewardship, tourism is up 17% from last year, resulting in a benefit to restaurants, hotels, and shops as well. Also, during this same time period, employment in Mr. Benton's businesses is up 4%, meaning new hires have also seen the benefit." The lawyer was on a roll and raised his voice accordingly.

"It is also a fact that Benton Manor, since it has become a tourist attraction, has not only shown a profit, and has employed more residents but is also contributing to the tax base. If that is the case, your honor, then one might argue the beneficiaries of the forgery happen to be the people, companies, and our local government helped the most by this crime." The lawyer paused and looked over towards Benton and his team. "Those people and businesses in the very town which bears the name of our illustrious benefactor, Mr. Harley Benton. Some who are now sitting in your courtroom!"

The judge looked on hiding an amused grin with his hand. Kennedy's lawyer, his head tilted and a finger in the air, looked for a response. Kennedy was expressionless and stoic as always. But it was the crowd that tipped the scales of justice. Each person in the courtroom glared at both Harley Benton and his lawyer.

Flack was looking to reach higher office in the coming year and saw his chances, along with the frowns aimed at him, sink lower.

"Counselor Flack, anything to add?" asked the judge.

Benton's lawyer rose. He looked at an angry Benton. If he said nothing, he'd be fired. He then looked out at the crowd. If he proceeded, chances of a higher office would disappear altogether. He chose termination. "Nothing further, Your Honor." Benton scowled but no one other than his lawyer noticed as all eyes moved onto the judge.

"Mr. Grange, you've presented an interesting case. A little unorthodox, but interesting. Therefore, I think this calls for an unorthodox ruling. It is thereby noted Mr. Kennedy has admitted to altering a document." The crowd gasped in unison. The judge waved a hand to subdue the crowd.

"However," he continued. "There are several factors in this case needing consideration. One, the town and its people and *not* the defendant were the beneficiaries of this crime. Two, the Benton companies have been managed wisely and profitably. Three, the defendant has no prior convictions, and lastly, there were no victims in this case. Therefore, it is my ruling to reduce the crime to tampering, a misdemeanor. By the state's definition of forgery as the alteration of a legal document with intent to defraud, there was *no intent* to defraud. In fact, Mr. Kennedy's actions failed to hurt Mr. Benton's estate, but instead enriched it. Mr. Benton should consider himself thankful he entrusted these men with his estate."

The judge took a deep breath and exhaled loudly. "Will the defendant please rise?"

Kennedy and his lawyer stood up. In solidarity, Axel joined them.

"Mr. Kennedy, forgery is a serious crime. One cannot go around signing another's name to documents as he sees fit. Even with the circumstances as laid out, State guidelines sentencing is a year in jail."

The crowd erupted in anger forcing the judge to use his gavel. "Order," he barked. "State laws *also* offer latitude to a wide range of penalties. Reducing the charge to tampering allows this judge to determine the most appropriate punishment. Because of the reasons stated before, my determination is three months in the county jail with no fines or restitution levied. Mr. Kennedy, I will give you one week to get your affairs in order. Then you will present yourself to the county jail to begin your sentence."

Flack tried one last ditch effort to save face. "What about bail? This man is a flight risk!"

Grange stepped in, "Your Honor, Mr. Kennedy is no flight risk. The man just pled guilty on his own accord and against legal counsel. Plus, he doesn't even own a passport."

The judge held up his gavel and addressed the soon-to-be incarcerated ex-butler. "Mr. Kennedy?"

"Yes, Your Honor?"

"Do you give me your word you will not attempt to flee and show up to the county jail next week to serve your sentence?"

Kennedy nodded. "I do indeed Your Honor. I give you my word."

"Then, I see no reason for bail. Motion denied. One week, Mr. Kennedy."

Benton growled from his table but the judge silenced him, bringing his gavel down. "Court is adjourned!"

The courtroom emptied rapidly save for the two opposing sides. Kennedy addressed Axel, "Thank you for your last-minute work. It saved me nine months. I wish you hadn't though."

"Brogan," Axel whispered. "You may not think you're worthy of your grandfather's name, but I disagree. I couldn't be prouder to call you my friend. It's not often we see someone take accountability for their actions these days. Your grandfather would be proud."

As they began to leave, they were confronted by Benton, a fierce look on his face. "Nah oveah yeht," he slurred at the two men.

"Did he say, 'Not over yet?'" Axel asked, a mocking tone apparent.

"I believe he did," answered Kennedy. He walked over to the old man and bent closer so Benton could clearly understand. "It is definitely over."

Benton made a gesture that Kennedy interpreted as driving. "Paren killah," he whispered.

Kennedy smiled at the old man. "Oh, Harley," he whispered in return. "Not even you are so stupid as to resurrect the accident to hold over my head. Did you forget that covering up this incident makes you an accessory? Who knows, maybe a jail cell would be an improvement over being stuck inside the Passing Lane, wouldn't you say?"

"I will geh my legger back. I will," the old man barked.

Kennedy nodded in agreement, explaining, "You can have it back. But you have to ask Chief Kepner for it. He's holding it for you." He then bent closer, whispering so only the old man could hear, "And don't worry about those pesky loans." Kennedy grinned at the last sentence. "I retired them all."

Harley Benton, not accustomed to being on the wrong side of any deal, stared back in disbelief, the rising anger coloring his face a bright red.

"Good luck getting it back!" whispered Axel, who gave Harley Benton a smirk as he and Grange ushered Kennedy toward the courtroom door.

"What's a legger?" Grange whispered to Kennedy. Both Axel and Kennedy laughed at the question. Grange shrugged his shoulders in confusion.

All three hoped their dealings with the old man were over, but knowing Harley Benton and what he was capable of, none of them could be sure.

On the way out of the courtroom, Kennedy looked for the Bulldog. The assistant chief was sitting in the hallway on a bench, his eyes focused solely on the ex-butler, a smug expression giving notice of his pleasure concerning the verdict. Kennedy looked away. *At least Axel was safe.*

Once in the car, and out of earshot, Axel turned to Kennedy. "Ok, how'd you do it?"

"Do what?" Kennedy answered.

"You know. How'd you get the judge to give you a lighter sentence?"

"Now young man, you wait a second. I was fine with spending a year in jail for my misdeeds. It was you who saved me from a longer sentence. Besides, the judge was probably just passing on a good deed to a neighbor."

"Not buying it," stated Axel. "I saw the look between you and the judge when the ledger was brought up. He looked worried until you shook your head at him. Is the judge in the ledger?"

Kennedy chuckled. "You noticed. I'm glad no one else did." What he meant was, he was glad the Bulldog didn't notice. "Yes, he was. But not in the ledger I gave to Kepner."

"So, what gives? What did you do?"

Kennedy took a deep breath. "Fine. All I did was confirm to the judge he didn't need to worry about his debt to Benton. There was no longer any proof of it."

"Wait, you approached the judge before you entered the courtroom?"

"I didn't," said Kennedy. "You did by mailing those letters. There was one addressed to the judge. I could tell he'd read it by how comfortable he was when Flack kept throwing out insinuations."

"So Judge Colson was on the list, huh? How did that happen?"

Kennedy snickered. "The judge has done nothing wrong. It seems that like me, Judge Colson is not a good gambler."

Axel raised his eyes in shock. "So, you let *me* give him the information that would alter his decision? You tricked me into a conspiracy! First of all, that is so not like you. Secondly, what did you do to guarantee there would be no proof?"

This was the perfect time for Kennedy to explain his process for retiring debt and destroying the pages he'd kept from the ledger. "No proof, no signature, no debt. And no leverage against a judge. Or anyone else on those pages, for that matter." Especially the deceased brother of Axel.

Axel scratched his head. "But that's leverage itself. You were acting like the man you despise."

Kennedy tipped his head to one side. "Perhaps. But the difference is I never asked for a favor. I was merely doing a good deed. Call it a public service. A present-day Robin Hood. Try as he might, Benton can no longer hold anything over the heads of the residents in this town again. Including a sitting justice."

"Oh," said Axel. "So, you destroyed all the pages you took from the ledger?"

"Let's not get crazy. The way I see it, we may need to enact additional public services in the future, don't you think? The less you know, the better. But now you have to answer my question. How did you know I was going to plead guilty?"

Axel shot a side glance at his friend before turning his eyes back to the road. "I didn't. But because you were adamant about me not being in the room while you forged Benton's name, I knew it was a possibility. I compiled the information out of caution. Plus, this was something an honorable man would do. Wasn't taking any chances."

"Boy scout," Kennedy said in jest.

"Scofflaw," Axel answered.

The two chuckled for a moment before turning solemn, realizing they had another important service to attend during the last week of Kennedy's freedom. They still had a pregnant Veronica to find.

⌒⊃

Veronica lifted her head, the creaking of the metal door disturbing her afternoon nap. How long had she been asleep? Would the guys be back this soon? She certainly hoped so. She was getting so tired of this bound and gagged scenario. At least she didn't have to wear that stupid sleep mask.

Sleep still held power over her eyes, temporarily causing a lack of focus. Tipping an ear towards the door, she heard footsteps too soft for her male captors. Her ears perked up. They sounded as if coming from a woman. An old woman.

Winnie stepped out of the shadows, "Veronica?" she whispered. Veronica squinted and drowned the urge to scream through the tape but managed a hoarse moan that caught the old woman's attention. Winnie softly pulled the tape from Veronica's mouth and whispered, "Are you OK?"

"Fine, I'm fine," Veronica whispered back as she stretched her jaw muscles. Regaining her vision, she looked around for the two goons. "Did you get abducted also?"

"What? No, I'm here to free you." Winnie began to pick at the knots on the ropes that bound Veronica. "Damn arthritis," she complained, shaking her hands before a second attempt.

"How did you find me?"

"Jules and I figured it out. If I had to wait for the police or Axel, you'd still have this tape on your mouth. Be quiet while I try to get this rope off. I'm afraid we don't have much time. I just got a text and your friends are on their way back. By the way, the drawing was a nice touch," she said, bobbing her head toward the window.

Veronica looked at the hard hat still atop the old woman's head. Winnie noticed and tossed it toward some boxes. It clattered as it slid behind one and out of sight. "Cover," she whispered, cringing at the noise. "Right now, we have to get you free."

Try as she might, Winnie wasn't strong enough to untie the knots holding Veronica to the chair. Her flaring arthritis didn't help. Looking around, she stated, "I'll be right back."

"Wait! Don't leave me!" Veronica whisper shouted, but it was too late. Winnie had slipped away, for what she wasn't sure. The old woman went to the kitchen area searching but returned with only a bottle of water. She opened it and gave Veronica a sip, replacing the cap before placing it on the floor. Veronica mouthed the word, 'Thanks.'

"I was looking for something to cut the ropes but couldn't…" Winnie's voice trailed off as the sound of a car was heard. She looked at her phone, then back at Veronica where she put a finger to her lips. "Uh oh," she whispered. "We have company." Picking up the water bottle and opening it, she poured the contents into Veronica's lap.

"What did you do that for!" she hissed, as the water soaked her nursing pants and began pooling underneath her chair.

"Vee, you're pregnant, so act like it," Winnie whispered back.

Understanding the ruse, Veronica said, "But I'm only seven months along. They'll never buy it."

"Honey, guys are so dumb when it comes to babies coming, they lose all sense of themselves." Winnie pulled Hector's Tag-It from her pocket and slipped it into Veronica's shoe.

"Insurance," Winnie whispered as she placed the tape back over Veronica's mouth. "Now stall a little to give us time to set the trap. These foxes aren't so smart," she finished, before receding into the shadows and silently making her escape through the back door just as the kidnappers entered from the other side.

Veronica heard the men before she saw them. "Showtime," she said to herself and began to moan through the tape to cover for Winnie's escape.

"Shut up, Grizz," Pinky said, as they approached.

"Two days we wasted. I hate getting stood up." Grizz scowled. "It's not a nice thing to do, is all. And I'm bored. I wish there was some type of excitement."

Veronica tried to smile under the tape; *You won't have to wait long to find it.* Then came another faux moan.

"So, how's our little card shark?" Pinky asked Veronica as he strolled up to her chair. "Get it Grizz? She was a little baitfish but turned into a shark!" Pinky said, proud of his joke. "You're lucky we couldn't find the old lady. She's out there somewhere, but we'll get her."

"Wonder if the old man is in?" Griff asked. Veronica answered his question with another moan. Winnie was right, they are dumb, Veronica thought. *Could I be any louder?*

Pinky began to peel the duct tape from Veronica's mouth. "What the hell?" he screeched as he stepped into the puddle that seeped from under the chair. Noticing the wet stain on the front of her scrubs, he asked, "Why are you all wet? Didja pee yourself?" And then turning to Grizz, said, "I told ya you should have taken her to the bathroom first!"

"My wawer bwoke," Veronica said from her half-taped mouth.

"What?" Pinky asked, ripping off the remaining tape. "What did you say?"

"Oww," Veronica squealed, then replied through clenched teeth, "I said, my water broke, you dimwits."

"Whoa, whoa!" said a surprised Grizz. "What are we gonna do?" Both men looked up at the second floor. "Hey up there," Pinky yelled. "You here? We got an emergency!" When he didn't receive an answer, Pinky bit his upper lip in thought.

Irritated, Veronica broke into the conversation. "Hey Shakespeare, there's only one thing to do. If you don't want all the messiness that goes along with playing a midwife, I suggest you take me to the hospital."

Both men stared at her. "NOW!" she yelled.

"Shouldn't we call an ambulance?" Grizz paced as he panicked.

"And give away our hideout? No way." Scrunching his eyes, he said to Grizz, "I didn't sign on for kidnapping AND delivering a kid. If the old man ain't here, I'm calling the shots. Get the car. We'll drop her off at the emergency room and hightail it out of town."

Grizz stood frozen, like an ice sculpture. Pinky defrosted him. "Either you get the car, or you deal with the placenta!" Grizz, faced with *that* choice, turned, and ran for the vehicle.

Pinky pulled out his switchblade and cut the ropes binding her wrists. He grabbed an arm and lifted Veronica from the chair. She moaned again and this time, touched her belly for effect.

"Hurry," she said, playing her role to perfection. "I think it's coming." She limped along as Pinky hurried her to the door.

"What's wrong with your foot?" he asked, noticing her limp.

"It fell asleep while I was tied up, you moron. Let's focus on what's about to come out of my soo-soo, shall we?"

This explanation seemed to not only placate but frighten the man. He began to drag her faster. "Hold on, we'll get ya to the hospital in time. Just don't mess up my car interior."

"Ooooh," came her mock cry of pain. Remembering Winnie's last instruction, she bent over to stall. "Give me a second," she said, as she took some deep breaths before walking towards the exit. Slowly

When Pinky wasn't looking and despite the discomfort of the Tag-It! in her shoe, she put a hand to her mouth hiding a very comfortable grin as she thought, Winnie is a genius. And right about guys. When it comes to female issues, they *are* stupid.

# Chapter Fifteen

From a parked car overlooking both the project site and the cement structure, the boss decided it was time to pull the last string on this tattered shawl of kidnapping. The purpose had been fulfilled and now the only missing piece was to make sure the pregnant lady was rescued safely and those two idiots took the fall.

The office had been wiped clean of any trace the boss had been there. Sitting on the passenger seat was a box with a microphone attached. The essential piece allowing for one's voice to change. The boss had a deep voice, but not deep enough to sound like an old man. The job was complete, the ruse had worked to perfection. Now that there was no evidence linking the boss to the crime, it was time to free the pregnant one. Picking up the burner phone, the police were dialed.

"Good morning. I'd like to report…" A quizzical look overtook the boss. A car pulled up and Winnie Ahearne got out and snuck into the construction site. *Wasn't she supposed to be with the two thugs?* Ending the call was the only thing to do while the next part of this drama played out, questions firing at a rapid pace. *Did the old lady think she could save the pregnant girl? And how did the Ahearne woman find her in the first place?*

The car passed the building and parked at the end of the parking lot, its motor still running. A finger tapped the chin in contemplation. *Interesting.*

The boss watched as the Ahearne woman exited the construction site and was looking intently at the cement structure housing the girl, before crossing the yard and entering through the closest door. *Unbelievable! Although she looks ridiculous in that white hard hat.*

Several minutes passed and a second car, the black sedan, approached the rear of the building, parking next to the cement structure. The two thugs got out and entered the building.

Pinky, the small one, was cursing up a storm. Seems the old woman pulled a fast one. *Am I going to have to go back inside?*

That question proved moot. The Ahearne woman was alone as she exited the structure from the far side door and ran through the construction site to the waiting vehicle which then sped off. Moments later the large man named Grizz came out of the building and got into the black sedan, starting it. A few minutes later, Pinky followed with the pregnant girl who struggled to hold onto his arm and with her other hand, held her belly, stopping every few feet. It took a while, but finally, they both entered the sedan and drove off as well. *What in the hell? That's not part of the plan.*

"Have to see how this all plays out," said the boss. The car was started and put it in gear, following the sedan at a safe distance, until it turned right into the Benton Memorial Emergency entrance. There was no sign of the Ahearne woman's car, but the sedan was followed by two of Benton Fall's finest unmarked cars. *Could this play out any better?* The boss drove slowly by, chortling, "No need for everyone to get arrested."

Winnie got back into the car as Jules tore out of the parking lot. "Hurry," she ordered dialing her cell. Once connecting with Kepner, she barked, "Sheriff? I have a present wrapped and ready to deliver to you shortly. How long will it take to get a team to Benton Falls Emergency?"

On the other end, Chief Kepner let the title comment go. He was confused until Winnie explained what was about to happen.

"Sweet Jesus," he stated, putting a hand to his forehead. "Are you sure about this?"

"Of course, I'm sure. I just put it into motion! And if you don't get there soon, those foxes will slip away."

"Foxes?" asked Kepner. "Winnie, are you ok?"

Winnie laughed, "I'm more than ok! This is the most fun I've had in years! We're on our way and will see you shortly."

"Wait, How did you pull this off?"

"Well, not through you," she stated. "Some investigative tactics do not deserve to be exposed to you, Sheriff. You may be good with your twenty-four-hour policies, but a bit soft on sheriffing."

Again, Kepner ignored the insult. He needed to focus on saving a kidnap victim and arresting the kidnappers. "Come in the back entrance, not the emergency one, so as not to spook the…foxes, as you call them," the chief cautioned.

"Kepner," Winnie responded. "I was born at night, but not last night." Then adding to show who the real boss was. "I was the mastermind to this whole shebang, wasn't I, sheriff?"

When she heard Kepner chuckle, she hung up. "Dolts," she said. Jules couldn't suppress her laughter.

Winnie then called Hector and gave him instructions to get to the emergency room as well. "Open your Tag-It! App and keep an eye on the green dot coming towards the hospital," she instructed. "If'n it changes directions, alert Sherriff Kepner."

Hanging up on Hector, she turned to Jules. "I guess it's time to let the guys in on the plan. I just know Axel will get his tighty whiteys in a bunch, but too bad. He was arrogant enough to think he was leading this old horse to water to make her drink. Well, I showed him, didn't I?"

"You surely did, Miss Winnie," Jules responded with another laugh. "You surely did!"

"Maybe those two will be drinking later on."

"Axel and Kennedy? Why is that?" Jules asked.

"They'll be hungry of course." Now Winnie was laughing.

Confused, yet giggling, Jules responded, "I'm not sure I follow but I'm sure it's hilarious!"

Jules was right, as Winnie gave her the punchline, "A bit of the Irish whiskey might help them choke down the words they're going to have to eat."

Both women cackled at the thought.

Winnie dialed again and put the phone to her ear as Jules raced to the hospital. "Axel? It's me, Winnie. We need the ransom note. Also, you got any whisky handy?" She began to explain but he cut her off.

"What? The ransom note I understand, but whisky? What are you up to, old woman?" Frustrated, Winnie groused, "For once would you shut up and listen?" She then explained the situation and his role in it. "And stay away from the emergency exit," she cautioned.

"As for the whiskey?" she added, "Once this is over, we're all going to need some. Especially you."

⌒

"Ooohhhhh," moaned Veronica. Believing she'd stalled long enough; she kept the ruse going knowing the two in the front seat wouldn't dare do anything but drive. Marveling at how Winnie had found her and then masterminded the plan to get her out of the building, she finally understood her comment on *insurance.* In the netting behind the driver's seat, she recognized the identical object placed in her shoe. *A Tag-It! like the one on her key chain!* Shaking her head in admiration, she whispered, "Only Winnie."

Both men turned their heads toward Veronica. Pinky shoved Grizz back towards the windshield. "You drive, I'll turn. Got it?" Then turning back to Veronica, he gave her a worried expression. "How's it going? Can you hold on?"

Knowing he was more concerned for his leather seats than her welfare, she dialed it up, bending in mock pain. "Hurry!" she cried. "PLEASE!" She tilted her head so he couldn't see the smirk on her face. Messing with these idiots turned out to be fun. Her reverse Stockholm Syndrome seemed to work freeing her from the chair, but Winnie's plan freed her from the building. The two thought they were in control, but Winnie proved otherwise. While her head was still down, Veronica glanced once again at the shiny object in the netting. She left the one in her shoe alone. Just in case. It was like putting two big red flags on top of the sedan.

Nobody, not even the police, could miss *that* signal.

⌒⌒⌒

Axel and Kennedy were going over maps to try and find a likely hiding place for the kidnappers but came up empty, discouraged because they were stumped. How could criminals hide in a small town like this? Especially with the technology of today? Drones, phone call taps, social media brags?

"Perhaps you were too hard on Winnie," offered Kennedy.

"This is no job for a frail old woman. I'm just trying to protect her," Axel responded.

Kennedy delivered an audible harumph. "She's not as frail… or old as you think. She's one sharp lady and has done a wonderful job at the FALM, hasn't she?"

Axel had to admit Kennedy's point. The FALM was in great shape. Winnie had effectively shut the door on the sordid hastening episode, encouraging residents to stay and bringing in new ones. The FALM was on the best financial footing in decades. But that effort went for naught now that she'd been fired.

"I just want to protect her," Axel said weakly.

Axel's phone rang. "Speak of the devil. What does she want now?" He answered, "Hey Winnie, what's up? What? The ransom note I understand, but whisky? What are you up to, old woman?" He paused as she told him the reason for the call. When she finished, he ended the call by saying, "We're on our way."

"My God, that woman will be the death of me yet!" Axel said to Kennedy. "She said Veronica was headed to the hospital with the kidnappers right now! Grab the ransom note. And remember, we just found it, right?"

The two men got up from the table, scattering maps in the process. Kennedy grabbed the car keys, and the ransom note from its hiding place before following Axel out the front door. "I'll drive."

In his hurry, Axel failed to close it. It wouldn't be necessary if what Winnie told him was true. The imminent capture of Veronica's kidnappers.

"Wait," Axel said, putting a palm to his forehead "I almost forgot something." He went back into the house and straight into the kitchen. He opened a cabinet, grabbed what he was looking for, and headed back to the car, this time pulling the door shut behind him, still unlocked.

Once in the passenger seat, he said, "She asked me to bring this. Said we're gonna need it. Not sure what she meant." In Axel's right hand, he held his grandmother's request.

A bottle of Irish whiskey.

Chief Kepner stood inside the entrance to the Benton Falls Emergency room for cover. Hector stood next to him focused on his phone screen, the green dot that showed Veronica's whereabouts moving toward them. The Tag-It! was doing its job by showing the path the kidnappers were on. Right into their trap. The Bulldog, standing next to a wheelchair, waited by the emergency doors dressed in surgery scrubs he'd commandeered from a hospital staffer.

Winnie and Jules came in through the hallway. Winnie, out of breath and wheezing, said, "I'm too old for this crap." She slapped her hands to her knees, took a deep breath, and then lifted her face to the men. "Have you got our girl?"

Both Hector and Kepner nodded.

"Good, but just in case they decide to drop her off early…" She stood up and showed the chief her phone and the green dot.

"Two Tag-It's?" he said, raising an eyebrow.

"Not takin' any chances with my soon-to-be-born grandchild." Winnie once again put her hands on her knees and took a deep breath.

"Great grandchild," Axel reminded her, as he and Kennedy sidled up to the group. Winnie noticed his bitter tone, perhaps still annoyed at being cut out of her master plan.

"Watch it boyo, or I might be inclined to let those goons take *you* for a ride."

Kepner broke in, "No need for that. Here they come."

The chief had instructed his deputies to seal off the exit from the hospital's emergency entrance. Once the kidnappers entered and dropped Veronica off, two unmarked cars would block them in and the trap set. The Bulldog was assigned to bring the wheelchair out to retrieve Veronica, thus the scrubs. When he questioned Kepner about his role, the chief told him, "Nick, I know your feelings about cowardly kidnappers and how you'd like to deal with them. My plan ensures the kidnappers go to trial and not the morgue." Disappointed, yet seeing the chief's logic, the Bulldog complied.

Winnie, still unwilling to take any chances, looked heaven word. "Blessed are the peacekeepers," she prayed, causing everyone to glance her way, smirks all around.

"It's showtime," Kepner said into his walkie-talkie. "Heads up."

The sedan flew into the emergency room entrance and slammed on the brakes. Pinky jumped out first and opened the passenger door for Veronica as the large orderly in scrubs brought out a wheelchair.

Veronica calmly walked over and sat down, smiling at the assistant chief, the faux labor pains no longer necessary. Both she and the orderly turned their gazes at Pinky, who wore a curious expression as he surveyed the area. "Wait," he said to the orderly, "How did you know…" Danger dawned on the smaller thug, causing him to dash to the car, cursing the fact he hadn't listened to his gut sooner.

"Get outta here, it's a trap!" he yelled. Grizz slammed the accelerator and the car jolted ahead in an attempt to escape through the exit. Unfortunately for the two kidnappers, a police car sat in its way, surrounded by several officers brandishing their weapons. Two unmarked police cruisers slid in to seal off a rear escape.

"Shit," was all Grizz could say as the two exited the vehicle and knelt on the ground, their hands raised in defeat. Pinky looked back at the people emerging from the emergency room as the police descended on them. Even lying down on his stomach, hands behind his back, he saw an old woman he recognized from the FALM. Their original target sported a smug grin.

Veronica walked over to the two thugs who had held her hostage with Winnie right behind her. An officer lifted the handcuffed Grizz to his feet, expletives spewing from his mouth directed at his former captive. Veronica turned to Winnie and said, "Winnie, if this asshat says one more word…" She never finished the sentence. Instead, she threw a right cross at Grizz, catching the kidnapper hard across the chin, leaving a red welt. He worked his jaw back and forth but remained silent.

Pinky yelled, "You gonna let that girl slap you?!?"

Veronica gazed at Pinky. "Girls slap. Hostages punch. Regardless of their gender. You better think twice before you kidnap anyone again. Especially a pregnant one." She lifted a fist and took a step towards Pinky. Reacting swiftly, he shuffled behind an officer's leg while lowering his head, tucking his chin against his shoulder.

"Coward," she said. Then looking at the police officer closest to her asked, "Did you get that?" He looked confused until she pointed to his body cam.

"Oh, yeah, got it all. Especially the punch. That was awesome! John Wayne couldn't have done it better."

"Good," she said, as she walked back to the wheelchair and sat down, her mission of humiliation complete.

The other officers pushed Grizz into a patrol car first, then attempted to do the same to Pinky. Driving away, his last glimpse would be of the old lady with hands on her hips, laughing.

The Bulldog was also laughing. A big and hearty bellow that caught everyone by surprise. The only thing worse than kidnappers were *free* kidnappers. And the Bulldog abhorred any kind of kidnappers, including dead ones. Even deceased, kidnappers were all cowards.

"How on earth did all this happen?" Axel broke in, still not sure how this rescue attempt played out.

"Chickens outfoxed the foxes," Jules said, grabbing Winnie's arm.

"Cock- a doodle- doo," crowed Winnie, kissing Veronica on her head. "So glad you're back safe and sound."

"Did I stall enough?"

"You did great. Just enough time for Kepner to get his team in place."

Turning to her grandson, she asked, "Axel, did you bring the whiskey?"

Axel lifted the bottle for her to see.

"Well, Cock- a doodle- doo," Winnie said again. "You do listen! Open it up and start drinking."

Axel didn't understand but did as he was told. The girls did, giggling at their little joke.

In all the outfoxing and the drinking down of eaten words, no one saw the lone vehicle slowly drive by the emergency exit. If someone had, they might believe it to be an interested motorist rubbernecking the unfolding drama instead of the brains behind the operation.

# Chapter Sixteen

Will and Harley Benton sat across from Carlton Flack as the lawyer was going over options when his secretary buzzed in Arabella. "Sorry I'm late. Had a last-minute emergency, but all's good now."

Will addressed his mother, "Will this take long? I have to get to work."

Arabella replied casually, "Oh, you have more important things to do. You don't need that job anymore. I sent Hector your resignation letter yesterday."

"You did WHAT?!?" Will said, incredulous. "I love the job! Why did you do that?"

"Relax," she said patting his hand. "We have bigger plans for you. Also, great news to share. For you too, Harley." She nodded her head at the lawyer, indicating she'd explain once they were alone.

Flack handed Benton the two signed documents and a check to Arabella. "Very generous," she said, her eyes widening. "Thank you. Very generous indeed."

To Flack, she ordered, "We need the room. Now."

Flack, visibly upset he was being thrown out of his own office, began a reply but stopped short. Benton had recently fired one lawyer and had come perilously close to firing him after the Kennedy trial. Flack chose to keep his client rather than his pride and left through the door leading into the reception area.

Arabella began, "Alright, let me inform you about what's happening now. It is unfortunate how Kennedy got off with a light sentence and the police couldn't pin anything on Ahearne, but the good news is we are in the clear."

Benton leaned in intent on hearing every word.

"Your Winnie is as sharp as you claimed. Right now, she is at the hospital with the pregnant girl. Both were fine the last time I saw them."

"Thucks?" Benton asked.

"That's the fun part. The two goons rode into a trap at Benton Memorial. Seems your friend, Winnie Ahearne knows how to effectively set one. Kidnapping is a serious crime and those two will be going away for a long time."

The old man leaned in conspiratorially. "Their friens?"

"Their friends?" Arabella said, patting the old man's hand. "They *have* no friends. But we do. Those two were never meant to get away. That's what happens when you piss off powerful people. You become conveniently expendable."

"Us?" Benton questioned.

"Us? We've done nothing. You were indisposed until recently in a retirement home. I've been working at the hospital as a nurse. And the old man the two kidnappers will say hired them? He'll never be found." Arabella lowered her voice as best she could. "As if he never existed."

"Wait a second," Will interjected. "What are you guys talking about? Kidnapping, pregnant girls, a man who doesn't exist?"

"Will, darling," said his mother as she once again patted his hand. "Don't you worry about a thing. Everything according to plan has worked out. Your father is free from that wretched old folks' home, his enemies have been neutered and you and I are here to help him rebuild his rightful place as the patriarch of Benton Falls."

Benton handed the first document to Will. His eyes widened as the realization appeared. He was being made executor of Benton's estate.

"Wait, you have this wrong. It says, 'Will Benton.'"

Smiling, the old man handed over the second document. It was a change of identity form filled out by the attorney.

"There are a few more steps to complete; Flack will help you," said Will's mother. She turned to Benton. "Wait till your nemesis sees the public notice. What I wouldn't give to see those expressions!" Benton gurgled a laugh.

"I still don't get it," claimed Will. "Why would you do this?"

Arabella took the documents and placed them on Flack's desk. He'd have to take over from here. "Dear, Harley isn't in the best of health. We want to make him comfortable in his remaining years. He and I both knew this day would come, we just thought we'd have more time. Once he had the stroke, we had to move forward."

"But why didn't you tell me he was my father before this?"

"Enemies," Benton answered. "Bah enemies."

"He was trying to protect you. But now you're older and it's time you learned from the best. He and I will groom you to take over the estate and claim your rightful place as the heir to the Benton name and fortune."

"But what about the other stuff? The kidnapping and the pregnant girl?"

Arabella waved a hand at her son. "Oh, relax. No one got hurt." Turning to Benton, she raised an eyebrow. He nodded his head for her to proceed. "Will, you have to take this to your grave. No one must know we were involved. The intention was to kidnap Winnie in order to lure Axel Ahearne back to Benton Falls. The pregnant girl was a mistake, but it worked just as well. Once Axel was back, we could try and prove the conspiracy to forge your father's signature on the will and put both he and Kennedy in jail."

"But why put them in jail? Why not just change the will and be done with it? You put yourselves in harm's way!" Will wrung his hands.

"Revense," snarled Benton.

Will cringed at the word. Benton was no longer the benevolent figure of Will's youth. He saw someone different. Someone dark, malevolent. The transformation frightened him.

"It's something you'll need to get used to, Will," said his mother. "Your fathers' enemies are now *your* enemies. If you don't destroy them, they will destroy you."

"WILL!" shouted Benton, before lowering his voice and speaking slowly. "Listen. Learn. Survive…Son."

Will let out a sigh. In the last few months, he'd found a job he loved and a new father. Now he faced a decision to trade the job in for wealth, prestige, a birthright…and enemies.

"Ok," he said. "If we're going to do this, I need a few assurances."

Benton sat back; his eyebrows raised. He lifted his right palm as if to ask, 'What assurances?'

"First," said Will. "No more shenanigans. You just came into my life; I don't want you going off to prison." Benton looked at Arabella before nodding his head in acceptance.

"Next, do not fire Hector Gonzales. He's doing a fine job and he is an asset to the FALM." Again, Benton shook his head.

"Third, let's leave well enough alone with the Ahearne's. The farther we distance ourselves from them, the less exposed we are." This time Benton paused, turning his gaze once more to Arabella. She lowered her head and raised her right eyebrow. Will missed the signal between the two as he waited for his father to accept his third demand. Benton complied.

"Good. That's settled," Will said happily.

Lifting a finger, as if to say, "Wait," Benton began writing on the notepad. After a few minutes of scribbling, he handed it to Arabella. "Your father wants assurances as well," she said to her son.

"First, you must pledge your undying loyalty to your parents. Secondly, you must be prepared to do what is necessary to protect us, the Benton name, and his assets. Lastly, you will find the right woman to marry and provide an heir to continue the Benton lineage."

To this directive, Will reacted with sarcasm. "Can I choose the girl? Or will you two do that for me?"

Arabella beamed. "I think we should make that decision by committee."

"But I get veto power, right?"

Both parents chuckled.

Will continued, "I need a job. Something to do while I'm learning the business."

"What do you have in mind?" asked his mother.

After Will told them of his idea, Arabella looked at Benton.

"Well, it is a start. Learn the business with first-hand experience and work your way up. And you to mentor him."

Benton nodded his approval.

"Is there anything else, your highness?" prodded his mother.

"Yes," Will answered, firmly taking his role seriously.

"What's next?"

Knowing his line of succession would continue, it was now Benton who beamed.

The old man adjusted himself in his chair. He spoke slowly and purposefully, "You playt your pawt welh." Benton had a slight slur but was intelligible enough for Arabella to understand him. "And I playt mine."

"Agreed. But now we have work to do. Once again, you have complete control of your estate and business interests. Your discharge papers at the FALM have been processed so we're ready to go home to Benton Manor. Both Will and I plan to move in to take care of you, We'll hire nurses on call twenty-four hours, a new staff, *and* you'll no longer have to worry about pesky tourists. How does that sound?"

Benton didn't need to speak. His smile said it all.

Will stepped behind the old man's wheelchair and leaning into Benton whispered, "Let's get you home where you belong... father."

Benton patted his son's hand before pointing ahead with two fingers aimed at the lawyer's oak door.

"Oh, so apropos. Onward," the new Will Benton stated, as he pushed his father through the door and into their future.

⌒つ

Nick Holmes, AKA the Bulldog, returned to the police station after scoping out the kidnapping sight. He walked straight to the chief's office, knocked on the door, and walked in without waiting for a reply.

"The old man is a ghost," he told the chief. "We searched high and low, swept the building. Forensics is there now. So far, nothing. Either those two guys are lying or we have one slippery character out there."

The chief scratched his ear before he spoke, "Can't catch ghosts, so I guess this will all be in your report?"

"Yessir," replied the Bulldog. "At least we have the two thugs. Have you alerted the Feds yet? They might have an interest in hearing what these two might have to say."

The chief nodded. "Way ahead of you, Nick. The Feds are sending an agent. Both men want to plead guilty. The bigger fish seemed too big for those thugs to rat out. They decided a prison sentence was a better alternative than what could happen if they squealed."

"Well, that's one good thing to come out of this," Bulldog said, frowning.

Kepner detected his assistant chief was disgruntled.

"Something you want to say, Nick?"

The Bulldog didn't hesitate. It wasn't in his nature to beat around the bush. He'd rather plow through it. "I can't believe we got outsmarted by that old woman. What right does she have playing detective anyway? Given a little more time, I woulda found the girl myself."

"May I remind you she not only found her but delivered the kidnappers right into our net. We should be thankful the woman had the sense not to listen to anyone. Including us."

The Bulldog remained sour until the chief offered him something to chew on.

"Hey, you want a new case?" he asked his assistant chief.

"Sure, what have you got?" The Bulldog raised an eyebrow in anticipation.

Chief Kepner reached into his desk drawer and pulled out Harley Benton's ledger. The Bulldog looked at it as a dog would view a bone… with meat still attached.

"We got all we needed up to this point but didn't have any more use once Benton was incapacitated. But now…" The chief didn't get to finish his sentence as the Bulldog grabbed the ledger and fled the office. If the Bulldog came up with any dirt on Benton, at least he'd know where to find the old man.

Having placated his assistant chief for the time being, Kepner's thoughts returned to the guile and bravery Winnie Ahearne exhibited. He picked up his cell phone and texted her an update.

It was the least he could do for her dogged determination to solve the case. He conceded he could use more of those traits in his police force. He shook his head clear of the thought of asking the old woman to consider working for him. Even though she would make a fine detective, he'd rather take his chances working with the Bulldog than have to spar with *that* woman ever again.

The day after giving their statements to Chief Kepner at the police station, the group assembled at Veronica's house. Kennedy made a pot of coffee and brewed tea. Winnie and Jules sat next to Veronica as she recounted the details of her abduction. Axel pouted in an easy chair.

"They really weren't that smart, were they," offered Winnie.

"Not really, and they didn't frighten me once I got to know them. A couple of big old bears if you ask me," added Veronica.

"What about the old man? The secretive boss from the second floor?" asked Jules. "Any leads on him?"

"The police are still investigating but Kepner indicated the man disappeared like a ghost. Didn't leave a trace. As if he wasn't real," stated Winnie.

Veronica bit her lip. "He was real to me. I might not have been scared of the two guys, but the old man frightened the bejesus out of me. I knew the other two wouldn't hurt me, but not so sure about the old man."

"When you testify at the trial, you'll have to tell them the truth," Axel interjected.

Veronica had a pensive expression. "That's what I'm afraid of. I don't want him coming back after me."

"Well, they'd have to come through me first. I'm here for the long haul." Winnie tilted her head before adding, "You know what gets my goat? After all this trouble, you'd think Kepner would at least say thank you!"

Veronica smiled, joking, "See what your good deed got you? On the other hand, I'd rather be the do-gooder than the unthankful ingrate any day."

"That's the difference between us," Winnie snapped, then whispered conspiratorially, "I was planning their demise…"

As the group chuckled at Winnie's joke, she was interrupted by a text on her phone. She read it slowly before looking up. "No need to fear. That was Kepner." She began to read aloud, *"Because of the overwhelming evidence, both men are willing to plead guilty to kidnapping so there won't be a trial. Thanks for finding the ransom note and for everyone's help in capturing the kidnappers. Especially you, Winnie."*

"Jesus, Mary, and Joseph. Looks like the rats aren't jumping ship after all."

Noticing everyone gawking at her, she asked, "What?"

Axel stepped in. "Winnie, weren't you just talking about not being thanked?"

Winnie blushed, "So?"

"Well?" Jules asked. "He thanked you. Aren't you going to retract your previous statement?"

"Hell no, I still don't trust them cops."

As the group laughed, she changed the subject, asking, "So now that everyone is free to do what they want, what are your plans?"

Kennedy entered the room with refreshments, including a bowl of pistachios and mustard for Veronica. "I will be detained for a few months so I'm considering my incarceration as a sabbatical. Perhaps I'll write my memoir. Or come up with a business idea. When released, I'll need another job." His comments brought down the tenor of the room. No one wanted to see him go away, but Kennedy was resigned to the fact penance was due and he was determined to pay it. He told everyone he had arranged for his surrender early so he could pay his debt to society and be done with it. But there was a more noble reason. Two to be exact. He hoped those two reasons remained where they were in time for him to gather important information.

"I'm told Hector will stay on at the FALM," said Winnie, changing the subject once more. "Seems as though Benton feels he's valuable. Not sure if Hector feels the same way, but a job is a job, I guess." Winnie breathed a sigh. "I'll miss the folks there, but not the job. I'm too old for the stress and too young to keep living there with the old fogies." Everyone chuckled except Axel. His scowl showed his continued displeasure.

Jules spoke up next. "We have to go back on the road pitching Leif's second book. Our publisher is anxious to see us back on stage. How many dates have we gotten booked so far, hon?"

Axel spit out, "Twenty-six. With another ten pending." He did not look the least bit pleased.

"Well, who pissed on your cornflakes this morning?" Winnie shook a finger at Axel. "You should thank your lucky stars you've got a great job. Do you know what people would give to trade places with you? Remember what the good book says, 'Pride comes before a falter!'" Even though she got the saying wrong, they all got the message.

Unsatisfied, Axel sat up in his chair. Instead of being grateful, he was defiant. "Anyone can have it after this next tour. I'm done."

"So, what do you think you'll do after the tour? Go back into accounting?" Winnie inquired.

"Hell, no!" he barked. "I have bigger plans. And they don't include any more of this detective cloak-and-dagger crap either. I'm done with that also."

"Atta boy," said Winnie. "Can't do anything about the past. Live with the presents you've been given."

Everyone looked at each other trying to understand Winnie's latest saying. Axel just shook his head. Jules broke the silence. Better than anyone, she knew Axel's capabilities.

"Alright tiger, settle down. First things first," she stated. "We're getting married!" She lifted her ring finger, but it was barren. This seemed to lighten Axel's mood. When Veronica and Winnie raised eyebrows, Axel jumped in.

"The ring is on the way, don't worry," he explained. "We're still in the planning phase. But she did say yes."

"Well, hurry up," said Winnie. "If you wait too long, I'll be attending the service in a casket, instead of sitting in the front pew!"

After the congratulations died down, all eyes turned to Veronica. Winnie had recently told everyone of Vee's plans but bound them all to secrecy.

"Now you can get back to planning your escape from Benton Falls. And to make it easier, I have a present for you. I even had it framed."

Veronica took the gift and unwrapped it. A wide grin crossed her face. "How?"

"Detective Kepner owed me a favor. Took it from the crime scene."

Winnie winced as Axel and Jules shook their heads and commented in unison, "POLICE CHIEF!"

Veronica ignored them as she walked over to the piano and placed the drawing on the lid, the bald-headed angel staring out at the group. "Perfect right there!" she said giggling.

Winnie looked wounded. "You're not taking it with you?"

"Dear heart," Veronica stated, "I'm not going anywhere. And miss all this fun? If this misadventure taught me anything, it's that I need my family more than anything. You," she claimed, waving a finger at each one, "*are* my family."

"What about what we discussed before? Your 'sadness?'" Winnie asked.

Veronica took a breath. "I've realized I'm a health care provider. I help people. I also know others who help people. I'll find someone to help me cope with my loss. There's no harm in asking when you need it." She lowered her head before adding, "And running away is no solution."

"From God's lips to my ears!" exclaimed a relieved Winnie.

Axel shook his head. "So, now God is speaking directly to you?"

"He better," Winnie shot back. "I'm the only one who knows what's going on around here. Besides, there is no longer a stigmata about getting the help you need."

Axel began to correct her. "Stig…" But Jules touched his arm and shook her head, which stopped him.

Everyone gathered around Veronica with words of encouragement. "Ok, get off of me before my water actually does break." She began to lift herself out of the chair when Kennedy offered a helping hand. "And when you return, mister," Veronica said, pointing at him, then Winnie "You are moving in here with me." Turning towards her savior, she added, "You are moving in today. There's plenty of room and I'll need both of you once the baby comes. But right now, I have to pee."

When she returned, Kennedy was standing at the front door. "It's time," he said. They all knew where he was going.

"Are you sure I can't give you a lift to the station?" asked Axel.

"No, the bus is fine. I'd rather we said our goodbyes here." In true Kennedy fashion, he held his head high, but his eyes gave away the sadness he felt on leaving his friends.

"Then take care of yourself and let me know if you need anything," said Axel. The two friends shook hands before Axel grabbed Kennedy and gave him a bear hug. Kennedy stiffened, not prone to such affection, then relaxed and wrapped his arms around the young man until Axel let him go.

Kennedy opened the door and waved, then stepped onto the porch.

Veronica yelled, "See you soon!"

Winnie followed her with, "Blessed are the merciful, for they shall receive mercy. May your jailers have mercy on you, Brogan Kennedy!"

Looking back into the doorway, Kennedy nodded at Winnie. Then he turned away and walked down the steps.

Winnie had finally gotten a Beatitude right. Kennedy had been merciful to her family, especially Axel. He'd also been merciful to those townsfolk indebted to Benton, freeing them from their burdens. And lastly, he had been merciful to himself, asking forgiveness of his sins not only from his friends but granting it to himself.

"If anyone deserves mercy, it's him," Axel said, pointing to the man walking down the driveway to serve his sentence. Axel rubbed the back of his neck. "There's one thing I don't understand," he said, addressing the group. "If Kennedy is going to jail, why do I feel as though I'm the one being punished?"

No one had an answer because they all felt the same.

Axel sat at the desk staring at the blank Word document, as if the empty page wished to mock him. A few nagging items arose. One, the task of working on the stage presentation for Leif's new book wasn't going to magically appear, and secondly, he should be happy now that Veronica was free, and Winnie was safe with her. But he wasn't happy. Not at all.

The good news mixed with the unpleasant. Harley Benton had returned home to Benton Manor. Also gone was the fortune Axel and Kennedy oversaw. Their efforts of last year trying to help the Benton Falls townspeople overcome years of treachery from the old man went for naught. Axel was disillusioned, angry, and perplexed at the unfolding events and believed he was at a standstill in his own life. There was, however, some relief to be finished with the whole mess.

Having acquired the overseer position through deception had never felt right. Justifying the means for the end masked his disappointment and guilt for letting Kennedy talk him into the forgery and then allowing the ex-butler to shoulder the burden of their crime by himself.

Kennedy would be fine. Once he got out of jail he would come back and protect Veronica, who needed him now more than ever. And he, Axel, still had a thriving business with Leif's estate and book sales, plus a woman who loved him. So why then, was he so miserable? Was it the loss of control of Benton's fortune? The inability to help the townsfolk? Or was it the sense of unfairness, that a man like Benton would once again exert his control over a town and its residents?

Deep down he knew those questions were part of the answer. He also knew there was a larger issue.

"Hell, the last few years would have made one hell of a book," he commented. Gazing out the window, he questioned, "Leif, where are you when I need you?"

Jules came in behind him, "Are you still moping? Is it because Winnie kept you in the dark?" she asked, hands on hips.

"You did also," Axel replied. Jules didn't like to see him this miserable and recently she didn't care much for his attitude, either.

"She swore me to secrecy. And you were being an ass. Frankly, I love you but I'm not sure I like you right now."

Axel stared at her. He knew she was bracing for his ego to emerge arguing that she was at fault. She was wrong. He dropped his head. "You're right. I have been an ass. All this time I've been trying to protect you both but what I should have been doing was listening. What you two did to find and then save Veronica was amazing. I should have been more empathetic."

Jules put an arm around him. "You've been the alpha dog during the last several months. I get it, it's been a foreign role for you. You've done well, stepping out on stage each night and keeping Leif's message alive. But it has changed you for the better and then again, not so much. You need to take what is good about the experience and delete what's bad about it. Going around being bossy and angry serves no one. Especially us."

Axel paused. He bit the inside of his lip in thought. He looked up at her and said, "So what's your take on what's next?"

"You really want my opinion?"

"Yes, of course."

"And you're not going to dismiss it?" She eyed him warily.

"No, I won't."

"Even if you don't like what you hear? Promise?" She leaned forward as an exclamation point after the question.

"I promise!" he said, his hands in the air in mock surrender. "I'll keep an open mind and a shut mouth."

"Good," she began, the alpha female emerging. "Then what you need to do is stop moping about. Control what you can and not what you can't. Tamp down the testosterone a bit. Remember, you and I are in a partnership. Not forty-nine to fifty-one or any other split other than fifty-fifty. Got it?"

Axel nodded his head in agreement. He also kept his word. He remained silent and listened.

Jules put a finger to her chin. "I know you're frustrated with the present situation. I am too. That's why I have an idea which could solve both our problems."

Axel listened intently as Jules outlined her idea. When she finished, he nodded in agreement. "I like the way you think. Now we have to sell Ted on the idea."

"He has no choice. The old publisher needs to come into the twenty first century where women have power as well. Remember, without us, Leif dies again. He doesn't want that. He may not be willing to walk away from his 'Golden

Goose,' but we are. And that is a powerful bargaining position." Noticing the blank page on the screen, she asked, "So, what are you trying to write, the new seminar?"

"Trying, but I keep thinking about the last year or so. All the things that happened, what we tried to accomplish, and Benton still wins in the end."

She ruffled his hair and when he ran his fingers through to straighten out the mess, she said, "Good thing you like to write. Authors can make their own endings, can't they? Not to mention the old adage, 'write what you know.'"

Axel turned to Jules and said, "You're absolutely right." Leif's words came back to him. *Self-help is the new religion.* Maybe his brother was onto something. Axel would always try and keep Leif's memory alive, but that didn't mean he couldn't follow his own path at the same time. Helping oneself was sage advice and writing what you know was a good place to start.

Thinking back on the last year, a title occurred to him. He began to type.

*A Good Mourning: A Benton Falls Mystery.*

"Oooh, I like that," cooed Jules. "Your wordplay is so sexy!"

Emboldened, he began to type out the first sentence from memory adding some descriptive verse.

*"I want an Irish Funeral," stated Winnie Ahearne, a comment to her grandson into the cooling air as if a thought not meant to escape her lips snuck its way out.*

"Winnie?" Jules queried. "You're writing about what happened last year?"

"Yup, it's a murder mystery. Winnie is a strong, interesting character. Don't worry, once I get the first draft done, I'll change the names to protect the innocent." He looked up at Jules and winked as he added, "And the guilty."

Jules put a hand to her chest in mock surprise, reminding him of his earlier claim. "I thought you were done with the cloak and dagger stuff?"

"I'm done with *living* it. Now I need to write about it. Haven't you heard? Truth is stranger than fiction."

"Well, you better paint me as a strong character instrumental in solving the case. If not, there might be a second murder mystery. An unsolvable one."

He watched as she turned and strode from the room. Words popped into his head. Not for the novel, but about his fiancé. *Beautiful, intelligent…and ruthless.*

Axel began to type again, freeing himself from the past by writing what he knew about it, typing his way into his own future. Jules was right. He needed to move in a direction *he* was comfortable with. Not to break away from Leif's, but to move parallel. And if Ted Holcomb didn't like it, tough. He would seek out a new publisher or better yet, publish it himself where he had more control. As he thought about sentences, character arcs, and plot holes, he began twirling the ring with Leif's ashes, hoping for inspiration. The rain had ceased and the sun had come out, sending a ray of light through the adjacent window and onto his laptop.

"Thanks, Leif," he said, observing the fitting punctuation mark on an otherwise gloomy few months before turning back to his laptop. This time, the blank page couldn't mock him. Axel's words flowed, filling it.

⟞⟝

Kennedy sat in his holding cell, patiently awaiting what was to come next. He was informed his lawyer was waiting to meet with him, but Kennedy refused. Justice was served and he would not be the one to undo the service, wondering if he would stay here in county jail for the duration or move to another jail. His wish was to stay close to home. He needed time to ferret out some information and to his credit, his decision to begin his sentence early was a sound one. The first part of his plan required the two men in the adjacent cell. He listened as they spoke. At first, it was in a whisper but soon became louder and more animated. "I knew something smelled fishy. My gut was telling me but I didn't listen," said the smaller of the two. "And if I ever get my hands on the old man, it's all over for him."

The bigger man responded sarcastically. "Right. What are you gonna do, throw your ring at him? You couldn't even take a punch from a pregnant lady, let alone handle an old man." Kennedy watched as the bigger man rubbed his jaw, recalling Veronica's right cross.

"Watch it, sasquatch. I'm plenty big enough to put a hurt on you myself."

The bigger man stopped rubbing his jaw and stood up, his fists raised in a boxing pose. "You wanna piece of me? Well, do ya?" he yelled.

"Gentlemen," interrupted Kennedy. "Looks like you two got played."

The big man spun menacingly towards the ex-butler. "Somethin' you wanna tell us?"

"Yeah," jumped in the smaller man, their fight forgotten for the moment, joining forces once again like squabbling siblings turning against a common foe. "What do you know about it?"

Kennedy, cagey so as not to play his hand just yet, answered, "Just an opinion, my friends. My assumption is that you're talking about the recent kidnapping. Am I correct?"

The two men looked at each other and then eyed Kennedy with suspicion.

"It's all over the news," Kennedy explained. "Hard not to know some things."

"You should mind your own business," said the smaller man.

"If you know what's good for you," added the big man.

"You're right, gentlemen. I should not stick my nose into how you could get out of this mess. My apologies." Kennedy moved as far away from the two thugs as possible without making further eye contact.

"Wait, what?" asked the smaller man. "Whaddaya mean 'get us outta this mess?'"

Feigning indifference, Kennedy responded, "Oh no, I'm afraid you were quite right. It's none of my business. Don't worry, I'm taking your advice." He turned and stared at the far end of the cell for effect.

Pinky rushed to the cage and stuck his nose through the bars. "Mister, if you know something that could help us, you had better start talking. We know dangerous men. *WE* are dangerous men," he said, correcting himself. "You don't want to get on the wrong side of this."

"But you told me to stay out of it." Kennedy had the thugs where he wanted them. "As for you knowing *people*, I have a question. Why aren't they helping you? And isn't that why you already pled guilty? These *dangerous* men?"

Grizz grimaced at the thought before speaking, "They are *too* dangerous."

Pinky put a hand to his forehead rubbing it slowly. Kennedy understood the smaller man was smart enough to know the answer. They were expendable to whoever hired them. And their so-called friends? It seemed to Kennedy the term 'friends' was a loose interpretation. Only God knew what orders *they* were given.

Pinky stuck his nose through the bars and softened his tone down to barely a whisper, "Hey mister, we're in deep trouble. You gonna help us or what?"

Kennedy resisted the urge to let the two know they had kidnapped his friend. The second part of his plan was to bury his own feelings and extract the information he needed. The plotters were still out there. Still free. And still a danger to his friends. It angered him to help these two criminals, but to eliminate the threat by finding those responsible proved more important and would better serve justice. Any information he could give the police would be just another form of penance so nothing like this would ever happen to his friends again. They needed protection at all costs.

"Are you sure you want to hear what I have to say?" When the thugs remained silent, Kennedy set the hook. "If you're sure?" he asked, his eyebrows raised as if asking his mother for forgiveness. Both men nodded.

Kennedy bit the inside of his lip so he wouldn't smile. Sometimes atonement came in the form of seeking justice. And in this case, retribution against the puppet masters pulling the strings on these two.

"Ok," he said, beginning his penance. "Let's start with how you got the job in the first place."

The new heir to the Benton name and fortune sat in the manager's office at the FALM. Events had happened so quickly that he'd hardly been able to catch his breath. He walked into the building as a visitor, became an employee and to his surprise, ended up running the place. He just hoped he was up to the task. He didn't want to disappoint his mother... or his father.

The office and its décor pleased the young man. He even had a private bathroom. He felt confident, almost powerful knowing he was in charge. The generous salary was a bonus. He'd never seen that much money in his paycheck before and daydreamed about what things he would buy first. But the salary was only the beginning. He was now the heir to the largest fortune in Benton Falls. Trying to get his head around that had been dizzying, yet he was getting used to the idea. He would have to work hard to show his worthiness.

Dottie's voice came over the intercom. It was flat and emotionless. "Will, your mother is on the line." The statement was followed by the click of her hanging up before he could acknowledge, causing his good mood to sour.

"Good morning, mother," he said into the phone. "She doesn't like me."

"Well, a good morning to you too. Who wouldn't like the handsome son of the great Harley Benton?" Her humor didn't help Will feel any better.

"Dottie is who. Every time she calls or sees me, it seems as though I just killed her dog. I don't know what to do."

"Oh, darling, of course you do. It's easy. You are the General Manager and have the power to do as you please. Just fire her and be done with it. Move on."

Will was aghast. Fire her? She'd done nothing wrong. She did her job well. The only complaint he had received was people thought her a bit nosy. And she hated Will. Neither of which were offenses requiring termination.

"At least Hector and I get along," Will offered. "It must be hard having an employee leapfrog you as your new boss."

"Oh, don't be so soft," his mother added. "It's time to buck up. I've been talking to your father and he doesn't like the numbers. Some residents have left to go elsewhere, intakes are down, and that means so are the revenues."

It was true. Once residents heard about the Ahearne woman's termination, some began transferring to other facilities. And intakes had all but dried up. Will suspected both were prompted by the fact that Harley Benton was once more in control of the business. He kept his suspicions to himself.

"Mom," he interjected. "A facility like this is where people come to, well, to die. We lost three residents from the Passing Lane last week alone. And I haven't hired a new marketing director yet because I can't find anyone with any talent to work for us. Can't bring in new clients without the right person."

"Will, with power comes responsibility. Harley believes you can handle this responsibility yourself so that hire has been put on hold for now."

The confident feeling of a few minutes prior was replaced by a small, uncomfortable weight in his stomach. "But Mom, I'm doing everything I can to keep up. I need help in recruiting new residents!"

"Will Benton, stop your whining right now." Will felt his mother's wrath building. It was suffocating. "You need to get a grip on the situation and handle it like a true Benton. Now suck. It. Up."

The nausea in Will's stomach grew. Grabbing his throat, he swallowed whatever vile thing was trying to come up. The term *interference* crept into his mind. He hadn't counted on this as a job requirement. They were supposed to guide him, not pull him along on a leash.

"I *will not* tolerate weakness. You've been given a gift, now be thankful and do your job." Anger was evident in her voice. Here was the "up to the task' and not 'disappointing his parents' yardsticks Will sought to avoid.

"And one more thing. Until the numbers rise again, your father and I feel it necessary to lay off the following people..."

Will scribbled their names onto a legal pad. This was not what he had signed up for. But if being the GM of this place meant bigger and better things in the world of Benton, he should take his mother's advice. The last thing he wanted was to go back to his previous life.

"I'm on it," he said.

"Good," replied Arabella hanging up. Will flinched recognizing his mother cut him off in the same fashion as his receptionist.

Sucking it up, he picked up the phone. "Dottie," he began. "Please arrange a one-on-one with the following three people today. And I'll need you to sit in each of those meetings."

After reading the names, he hung up. "One more reason to make Dottie hate me," he muttered, again feeling a strong urge to vomit. The only bright spot was that he had his own private bathroom so no one would ever know.

Backstage at the civic center, Axel paced. "Don't forget. Look for a smiling face, it will calm you down."

A chortle came from Jules. "I'm calm. But you. You're a nervous mess. Take a deep breath, will you?"

Jules was right. Axel was nervous. But not for himself. He had stood on stage numerous times in the last year, entertaining and educating those followers of Leif's 'self-help is the new religion' dictum. Today, he would not be going on stage. Today it was Jules's turn to step out of her old role for a new one. To walk out center stage and deliver the gospel according to Leif. Axel hadn't delivered a eulogy since these talks had begun. He didn't have to. Each seminar was an homage to Leif himself. And never a last word.

"How can you be so calm?" he asked.

She chuckled. "Oh Axel, I've watched you for so long, I could do this in my sleep. Besides, it's going to be fun!"

Kissing his cheek and throwing a wave, Jules walked onto the stage with purpose. With confidence. She pointed to someone in the audience, then turned toward Axel, her hands raised palms up and a shoulder shrug as if to say, "See? Easy."

She found a smile, he thought. His jitters faded as she began to speak. No stutters, no faltering, no sign of nerves. Just the image of what she was destined to do. He felt proud she'd come a long way from the shy girl working at the FALM. Now she took control of the audience.

"If you were expecting Axel Ahearne, surprise!" she blasted, raising her arms. The crowd responded with enthusiasm. One rule of public speaking- *enthusiasm begets enthusiasm.*

She flashed her ring towards the crowd. "Axel is my fiancé and I called Leif Ahearne my friend. Now I hope we can be friends as well. So, let's begin, shall we? My friend Leif wrote two books. *Climb Your Own Tree*." She waited for the applause to die out before finishing. "And now…" She held up Leif's second book, *Add More Leaves*.

As Axel watched, he beamed with pride. Not only was he lucky enough to marry her, but he also noted his bride-to-be was very good at this speaking gig. Even better than he was. No trace of jealousy or ego pains present. Her idea of them switching roles was brilliant. They were now in sync with their career paths. She added a branch onstage, and Axel's was added through his fiction writing. Best of all they could keep the promise. Leif's legacy would continue.

It was not just his time to climb. If he could climb, why couldn't she? With new branches they'd created, their tree was big enough for both to climb. Together.

As news of the heir to Benton's fortune reached Winnie, she found she wasn't shocked. After all, God had said, "Go forth and multiply." Benton had taken him seriously. Winnie wouldn't be surprised if there were more Benton spawn running around.

The second thing that came to mind was a dangerous word. Protégé. This fact did shock her. Knowing what kind of monster the father was, she could only surmise he would teach the son to be equally evil.

Winnie was exhausted from all the excitement of a rescue operation so after lunch as Veronica napped, she tried to relax for the first time since, well, she couldn't be sure when. Axel and Jules had left to resume their work on the road, and Kennedy sat in the county jail. Because the two guilty-pleading kidnappers were remanded into custody, discussions with the Police Chief and his assistant were no longer a necessity.

Relieved she found herself alone, Winnie plopped in a parlor chair, a tumbler of Irish whisky sitting next to her on the small table beside the lamp. All was quiet until a thought disturbed her worn-out mind.

The kidnappers may have been apprehended, but the motive was still unclear. Questions on why anyone would want to abduct an old woman or a pregnant one swirled around like a dust devil in the desert, partially transparent and opaque at the same time. Suspicions grew concerning Harley Benton, the only person who had a grudge to bear against her and her grandsons. Up until recently, that thought would have proved worthless. But now that he had regained his speech and partial mobility, his involvement made more sense. The question now was, 'How to prove it?' The two kidnappers were of no help, maintaining a silence that spurred rumors that they feared for their lives if they ratted.

And if not Benton, then there was a person or persons still out there. Still a danger. And if that was the case, Veronica needed a guardian angel.

She shook the thoughts away and took a sip of the whisky. "Ah, a touch of the Irish is just the remedy."

As weary as she was, and how comfortable the chair felt, she couldn't help noticing the home was in dire need of cleansing. Kennedy had been too busy to clean properly during the search for Veronica. Winnie couldn't fault the man for that, even though he and Axel were on the wrong track and hadn't found her, she appreciated the effort.

Pulling herself from the chair was a chore as her back screamed in pain. She took a deep breath before seeking out her first cleaning task. The upright piano reminded her of those from old Western movies. It was dusty and the music disheveled so she thought she'd start there.

Fingerprints lay on the lid proving someone had recently looked inside. She grabbed her drink to take another sip. "Needed some energy," she convinced herself, then went to the kitchen and found some furniture polish and a clean cloth.

Returning to the parlor, she began to polish the piano, moving Veronica's drawing, and replacing it to a clean spot. Wiping the fingerprints away, she then stacked the errant note music into a neat pile on its stand. Fatigue made her sit down on the piano bench to rest where she began to plunk the keys at random. She never learned how to play the instrument, which was Veronica's thing, having purchased an old used one when she moved into Winnie's house.

As she plucked, a sour note caught her ear. Remembering the fingerprints, she thought of reports of valuables found hidden in old pianos; a rare baseball card, a bag of gold coins, or a stash of cash.

Curious, she opened the lid and peered in. At first, she found nothing. She hit the note once more and saw the felt barely striking the string. Reaching behind it, she felt around until her fingers brushed paper. *What on God's green earth?*

Try as she might, she couldn't dislodge the paper without tearing off a piece. So as a precaution, she investigated the insides of the piano wherever she could reach but found nothing more.

Putting the lid down, she went around the piano, running her hands along the sides and back to see if a panel would open. She needed to get closer to the paper lodged inside.

Sitting back down on the bench, Winnie pressed along the edges of the foot pedal panel to no avail. Just when she was about to give up, one edge creaked open.

"Darn," she exclaimed. "Veronica is going to kill me." She tried to repair the damage but the panel continued to loosen. Checking more closely, it occurred to her that she hadn't broken the piano at all, just loosened a piece already displaced.

Gingerly, she worked the panel off and laid it to her right. She lowered her head underneath the keyboard. Sitting to the left of the pedals and wedged against the metal frame sat a book.

Releasing it from the frame, she placed it on the piano lid and tried to replace the knee panel to its original position. Frustrated, she leaned it against the piano, growling, "I'll deal with you later."

Forgetting about the piece of paper, she took the book back to her chair, taking another sip of whisky. Someone had taken the time to take a book and make a copy. Recognizing Axel wasn't that clever, she remembered Kennedy had handed over a special type of book to the authorities. She was certain the ex-butler had photocopied the book. That's wrong, she thought. *It's not a book.* Having worked in her own restaurant for years, she recognized what its contents spelled out to her. *It's a ledger.* Could this be a copy of *that* ledger?

The thought made her gulp the remaining alcohol. "Holy Heavens," she whispered, as the understanding she may have found the connection she sought.

She was aware Harley Benton's original ledger was in the custody of the Benton Falls police department, but these pages looked awfully like pages from that document. And if this ledger was a copy of the original, these pages would prove more valuable than one hundred old baseball cards or gold coins. It could also prove to be his downfall. Or at least a safeguard against him. She reminded herself to probe Kennedy when she went to visit him.

Winnie took a deep breath, thinking she'd need to get another taste of whiskey. Was she up to the task of battling the great and powerful Harley Benton? Or the old man from the kidnapping? Or both? She wasn't so sure.

"Snap out of it, old woman," she said, steeling her nerves. Her weariness dissipated with the newfound knowledge, replaced with adrenaline. "You don't have the luxury of being tired. Not when the stakes are this high." Winnie stood up and straightened her spine, determined to stay vigilant.

Wondering if her family could be kept safe, a saying came to mind. "Forewarned is forearmed." Winnie prayed to God, being forewarned would be enough. But just in case, she hedged her bet on being forearmed as well. Once Veronica was home safe and sound, Winnie had purchased a nine-millimeter handgun with the intent of taking firing lessons and a gun safety course. In addition to the weapon, she purchased a box full of hollow point bullets. The store clerk made a lot of sense when he informed her, "If you shoot an invader with these, you don't have to worry about the bullet going through and damaging a door or wallboard. The bullet stays inside and creates all sorts of havoc." The best part was the color of the gun. Pink. Smirking, she reasoned no criminal in their right mind wanted to get shot by a pink gun-toting geriatric woman. How would that look to their macho criminal friends? To them there would be nothing more embarrassing, she pondered.

She had her resolve, a weapon, and now Benton's ledger. Were self-defense courses next?

"Jesus, Mary, and Joseph…" she stated with conviction, knowing full well that only death could put a stop to her watch. But until then, she was determined to become that guardian angel, halo or not. This would be her new job. Always vigilant, always on guard against any and all threats. And never again any complaints of being too tired, too old, or too scared to protect her family.

Especially the precious, bald-headed angel soon to make its way into their world.

# Acknowledgements

I'd like to thank my beta readers, Eileene Dillman, Richard "Dutch" Ireland, and Jean Ball for their valuable feedback. Every writer should have readers as insightful, honest, and forthcoming as all of you.

Special thanks to Kimberly Martin and her team from Jera Publishing. From final edits and formatting to cover art, she and her staff are so easy to work with, always bringing my ideas to life!

Thanks to all my readers. I write for you and hope I keep you all entertained! You keep reading and I'll keep making up stuff!

And last but not least, thanks to my darling wife, Cynthia. Your love and support mean the world to me!

# Biography - Brian DeLaney

Brian is a former Advertising Executive with years of marketing and creative messaging experience and is member of the Atlanta Writers Club. He writes because he likes to make up stuff.

Brian lives in Alpharetta, Georgia with his wife Cynthia and near children Kelly, Kirstie, and Samson and their families. Together they enjoy traveling and frequently visiting their grandchildren. Brian also enjoys camping, kayaking, yard work, and playing his guitar. This is Brian's third novel.

9 798985 257847